The Switch

The Switch

Elmore Leonard

Copyright © Elmore Leonard, 1978

First published in Great Britain 1979
by Martin Secker & Warburg Ltd

Published in Large Print 1994 by
Isis Publishing Ltd.,
55 St. Thomas' Street, Oxford OX1 1JG,
by arrangement with Martin Secker &
Warburg Ltd.

All rights reserved

The moral right of the author has been asserted

Cataloguing in Publication Data for this book
is available from the British Library

ISBN 1-85695-312-2

KIN... ON THAMES
PU... RARIES
6/96
02458624
ALL
ST LP
CAT REFS
BNB
1395

For Mom and Another Mickey

Comm. 25/4/17

1

Mickey said, "I'll drive. I'd really like to."

Frank, holding the door open, said, "Get in the car, okay?" He wasn't going to say anything else. He handed her his golf trophy to hold, walked around and tipped the club parking boy a dollar. Mickey buckled the seat belt — something she seldom did — and lit a cigarette. Frank got in and turned on the radio.

They passed the Bloomfield Hills Police Department on Telegraph, south of Long Lake Road, going 85 miles an hour. Someone at the club that evening had said that anybody coming from Deep Run after a Saturday night party, anybody at all, would blow at least a twenty on the breathalizer. Frank had said his lawyer carried a couple $100 bills in his penny loafers at all times just to bail out friends. Frank, with his little-rascal grin, had never been stopped.

The white Mark V — washed daily — turned left on to Quarton Road. Mickey held her body rigid as the pale hood followed the headlight beams through the curves, at 70 miles an hour, conservatively straddling the double lines down the middle of the road, the Mark V swaying slightly, leaning — WJZZ-FM pouring out of the rear speakers — leaning harder, Mickey feeling herself pressed against the door and hearing the tires squeal and the bump-bump-bump jolting along the shoulder of the road, then through the red light at Lahser, up the hill and a mile to Covington, tires squealing again on the quick turn into the street, then coasting — "See? What's the problem?" — turning into the drive of the big brown and white Tudor home, grazing the high hedge and coming to an abrupt stop. In the paved turn-around area of the backyard, Frank twisted to look through the rear window, moved in reverse, maneuvered forward again, cranking the wheel, reverse again, gunning it, and slammed the Mark V into the garage, ripping the side molding from Mickey's Grand Prix as metal scraped against metal and white paint was laid in streaks over dark blue.

"Jesus Christ, you parked right in the middle of the garage!"

Mickey didn't say anything. Her shoulders were still hunched against the walled-in sound of scraping metal. After a moment she unbuckled and got out, leaving Frank's golf trophy on the seat.

It was cold in Bo's room. The window air-conditioner hummed and groaned as though it might build to a breaking point. Mickey turned the dial to low and the hum became soothing. In the strip of light from the door she could see Bo, his coarse blond hair on the pillow, his bare shoulders. His body lay twisted, the sheet pulled tightly against the hard narrow curve of his fanny. Mickey's word. Part of a thought. Practically no fanny at all, running it off six hours a day on tennis courts and developing the farmer tan — she kidded him about it — brown face and arms, white body. He didn't think it was funny. It was a tennis tan and the legs were brown, hard-muscled. He didn't think many things were funny. He would scowl and push his hair from his face. Now his face was slack, his mouth partly open. She kissed his cheek and could hear his breathing, her little boy who seemed to fill the twin bed. Bo would be fourteen in a month. "Going on thirty-five," she said to Frank. Only once. Frank had given her a tired but patient head-shake that was for women who didn't know about the concentration, the psyching up, the single-purpose will to win that a talented athlete must develop to become a champion. (Sometimes he sounded like a Wheaties commercial.)

She said, again only once, "What difference does it make if he wins or loses, if he's having fun?" Knowing it was a mistake as she said it. Frank said, "If you don't play to win, why keep score?" (Did that follow?) He then gave an example from the world of golf that drew only a vague parallel. Something about his second-shot lie on the 5-par 17th — the dog-leg to the right? — where he could chip out past the trees, play it safe; or he could take a wedge and if he stroked it just right, to get his loft and a little kick, he'd be sitting pin high. "You know how I played it?" Mickey, showing interest: "How?"

An unspoken house rule: Never talk about Bo if it's anything that might upset Frank. When the lines from his nose to his jaw tightened, stop. Switch to Bo's overpowering forehand. Or let Frank describe his day's round of golf, the entire eighteen, stroke by stroke. Keep the peace. Though the tiny voice in her mind was beginning to ask, louder each time, Why?

It was a pleasure watching Bo sleep. It was a pleasure watching him eat. It was a pleasure watching him play tennis when he was winning. But it was not a pleasure simply to be with him and talk. Frank said, "He's thirteen years old, for Christ sake. What do you want him to talk about?"

Coming into the bedroom with a drink and his golf trophy, Frank said, "You know, it's funny, after fifteen years I still have to explain to you this is *work*, winning this thing. You make remarks like it's a piece of shit."

Mickey was already in bed in her long white pajama top, her face scrubbed clean of eye-liner and lipstick; but he'd caught her. The bed lamp was still on.

"What'd I say this time?"

"You made some remarks at the table; I heard you."

"I said it looks like the Empire State Building

with a golfer on top."

"That's very funny."

"Well —" Mickey thought about it a moment. "How about the City National Bank Building?"

No, that was wrong; she should keep quiet. Frank was glaring at her, those little glassy eyes glaring away, the lines in his face drawing tight. Now he would either blow up or hold back and sound solemn.

"I'll tell you something," Frank said. He held the trophy high with one hand, showing her his strength as well as his reverence for the award. "Winning the club championship, bringing this home every year if I can do it, and I mean it takes *work,* is as important to my business as anything I do." He was having trouble holding it up.

Mickey said, "And the blazer with the club crest —"

Frank tensed. "You want to make fun of that too?"

"All I meant, it's another prize, something important to you."

"All you meant —" He turned away with the trophy and the drink and placed them side by side on his dresser. "All you meant, bullshit. That little innocent voice, Christ. All you do, you've got a way of putting everything down. You don't like the coat, you don't like the club crest on it. What else? The trophy —"

If she hadn't washed and brushed her teeth — if she'd turned the bed lamp off right away — She had thought Frank might stay downstairs awhile, watch a late movie with a drink and one eye closed.

"I asked you what the crest meant," Mickey said. "How long ago was that? I haven't said a word about it since."

"No, you haven't said anything —"

He was unbuttoning his shirt, showing her his chest. He did have a good chest. But a little too much stomach after all the drinks and dinner and after-dinner drinks; the stomach straining against the white patent-leather belt that matched his loafers. Frank liked matching outfits. For the club he liked paisley pants with a yellow or lime-green sport jacket. He owned twenty-five suits. Men who sold them would show Frank the latest "in" styles and he'd buy them. He parted his dark straight hair on the right side and wore sideburns that came to points. He was neat, an attractive, masculine-looking man; not tall, but well built, good chest and shoulders. He smiled easily; he knew almost every member of the club by name. He grinned and punched shoulders and called his golf buddies "partner." His voice was easily identified in the locker room and he was known to tell jokes well. Sometimes Mickey thought he was funny.

But she never felt *with* him.

Even now she was perched somewhere looking down, a spectator, watching the two of them in a pointless scene. Thinking of lines she could give herself, zingers; but knowing he would either get mad or not get it at all. So usually she backed off, played it safe and continued to watch.

He was still delivering broad sarcasm.

"You never say anything that people know what you're talking about. You realize that? You pull all this cute shit. Cute little Mickey Dawson; oh my, isn't she a cutie? She's fucking precious is what she is. Skinny little thing, nice boobs. How does she keep her figure? Those fat broads're always asking you that, right? Making comments? Well see, what she does — anybody wants to know — she concentrates on her husband, watches him like a fucking hawk so she can count his drinks. See, she gets so wrapped up in it, her cute little brain working away, counting, it burns up energy.

"She's just a cute little bundle of energy, counting drinks, running out to the club every day, taking Bo to matches, very devoted." He paused to take his drink from the dresser and finish it, defiantly. "Okay. How many did I have tonight?"

She had never thought of herself as cute little Mickey Dawson. She had come to accept people telling her she was cute — tired of acting surprised and discounting her looks. She preferred to think of herself as natural looking — with her Revlon Light 'n' Lively hair worn fairly short, barely teased and parted on the side — and with an inner something — she hoped — an awareness, that showed in her eyes, if anyone bothered to look. (The club lovers looked and saw their own reflections.) One thing for sure, she never *felt* cute or worked at it with cute moves.

"How many did I have. Come on."

"How many drinks?"

"Jesus Christ, I believe that's what we're talking about." Frank held his shirt open, waiting for the answer.

What was that supposed to do to her?

"I don't know," Mickey said. "I was there a half hour before you came out of the men's grill."

Frank unzipped his fly and she thought he was going to expose himself. "Okay, I had two in there, maybe three. How many more, after I came out?" He took his pants off, his back supported against the dresser. Still, he lurched as he threw the pants across a chair. "You counted them, didn't you?"

She was thinking: Take pictures of him sometime with the movie camera. Or have his tape recorder turned on and play it back in the morning. First, a tape of his nice-guy speech accepting the trophy, straight-faced, but with the hint of a boyish grin. ("I owe it all to clean living, a devoted wife and my opponent's double bogey on the fifteenth.") Then play the bedroom tape, the other Frank Dawson. He did not seem complicated; he played obvious roles. He was considered bright, but was actually very unaware. It would never occur to him that his wife was more intelligent than he was. Frank was the man, he was successful in business, he owned a $260,000 home, he played golf with a three handicap. (And she was the wife.) Maybe that's all there was to him.

She said, "I guess you'll drink as much as you want."

"Come on, how many did I have?"

"But I'm not going to drive home with you any more when you're drunk." There, she said it.

"Wait a minute. Now you're saying I'm drunk?"

Frank watched her close her eyes, face shining clean, hands folded over the neatly turned-back sheet. He walked over with the trophy, raised it and slammed it down hard on the empty flat side of the king-size bed. Mickey's eyes opened abruptly and she came up on her elbows as the trophy struck her legs, bounced awkwardly, and went end-over-end off the side of the bed.

Frank waited. After a moment he said, "I didn't mean to do that, but goddamn-it I'm asking you a question. You accuse me of being drunk, how many did I have?" Subdued, but hanging on.

Mickey was sitting up, touching her shins. They hurt with a throb, but she didn't want to push the sheet down to look.

"Aren't you?"

"Aren't I what?"

"Frank, why don't you go to bed?"

She lay back again, this time turning to her side, away from him. Reaching up to turn off the lamp, she saw the golfer on the floor, no longer on top of the Empire State Building.

Frank said, well, he counted them. She was always saying he should count his drinks, right? Well, tonight he'd counted them. He'd had eighteen since finishing golf at 6:30. Okay, now what was he supposed to do? You count drinks and then what? What was supposed to happen? Mickey didn't answer. You keep a record, is that it? What was it supposed to tell you?

At twenty past four Mickey heard her husband get up to go to the bathroom. She heard a bumping, scraping noise and raised her head to see Frank — a pale figure in the dark — pushing his dresser away from the wall, struggling with it, grunting, then wedging himself in behind it. There was silence before another sound came to her, soft and steady, as the Deep Run Country Club First Flight champ urinated down the wall and onto the oak floor.

After that, for awhile, she lay awake and asked herself questions.

What had they really been talking about? Not drinks. Why did she let him — Why did she play games with him? . . . Why was she afraid to tell him what she felt? Why didn't she cut through all the words and get to the point? . . . Why did she do things — sit around the club, smile, laugh at things that weren't funny — she didn't want to do? Playing kissy-ass, that's what it amounted to. Why was she so goddamn nice all the time? Nicey-nice. God.

2

Ten to nine, Sunday morning. Mickey, in a plain white scooped-neck tennis dress, stood at the kitchen counter with a cup of coffee and the Sunday *Detroit Free Press* — the linoleum floor cool and a little sticky beneath her bare feet. She had showered and was hungry, but would hold off the bacon and eggs until Bo came down.

She flipped through the sections of the thick Sunday edition — from the front-page headline, *Witnesses Finger Teen Gang Leaders* . . . past Sports, *BoSox Rout Tigers 10-2* . . . to the Women's Section, and stopped. God, there it was. With pictures.

TENNIS MOMS
Children's Games Become Their Career

The story, covering the entire first page of the section, was illustrated with five action shots of moms and their kids: the kids swinging tennis rackets; the moms staring, chewing lips, one smiling. Mickey saw herself, slightly out of focus, beyond Bo's clenched jaw, racket chopping down hard. The caption read: "Bo Dawson smashes a volley while his proud mother, Margaret 'Mickey' Dawson, watches from the sidelines. Bo's home court is Deep Run Country Club."

Her gaze scanned the columns of type, stopping to read about a mom who had canceled a trip to Europe in order to take her son to the Ann Arbor Open.

A Grosse Pointe mother had persuaded her husband to buy controlling interest in an indoor tennis club, then moved in as manager to promote her daughter's career full time.

Nothing about Bo's mom yet.

A Franklin Village mother, whose husband was in cardiac care at Sinai, told a friend, "I've lived my whole life for this (Southeastern Michigan Junior Championship). My husband isn't conscious; there's nothing I can do for him. But I can be with my daughter and help her."

In the third column, mothers were sweating out their children's matches, nail-biting, chain-smoking. There it was . . .

"Watching her son Bo in a match at Orchard Lake, Mickey Dawson claimed she wasn't the least bit nervous. Except there were 10 menthol cigarette butts at Mickey's feet by the end of the first set."

. . . Thrown in with the rest of the clutched-up tennis moms. She had told the relaxed young woman writer she *wasn't* nervous, not at all, and was sure she'd smoked no more than four or five cigarettes. The other butts could have been there before. If she had smoked ten — it was possible — it had nothing to do with Bo. Frank had been there too, growling, calling shots, officiating for the people in the stands.

There were quotes from moms agonizing: "Oh Kevin, oh Kevin, oh Kevin, please — that's it, baby. That's my baby."

Another one: "If only I had been there. Missy needed me and I let her down."

A mom complaining, her voice breaking: "They've got the seeding all backward. I can't believe it."

Rationalizing: "You start to figure if you combine your intelligence with your son's ability you can go all the way."

A minimizing mom said: "Not me, I have a husband I adore, I love to party, travel . . ." Her husband: "Any time you ask her to do anything, she has to check her calendar to make sure Scott doesn't have a tournament."

"Bo's father, Frank Dawson, shaking his head, but with a merry grin on his handsome face:

" 'If I told you what it cost a year, would you believe six, seven thousand?' "

". . . a merry grin on his handsome face." Frank loved to say "would you believe." He loved to talk about money, what things cost.

At five to nine, though, he didn't seem ready to talk about anything. Frank came into the kitchen wearing his yellow golf outfit and carrying an old pair of loafers, his eyes watery, glazed.

"You didn't call me."

"I didn't know you were playing."

"I never play on Sunday, uh?"

"I mean this early. You didn't say anything."

"We've got a 9:30 starting time. Overhill and some guy that works for him."

"Who's Overhill? Aren't you gonna have coffee?"

"No, just some juice, tomato juice. You know him; we had them out last year. Larry Overhill, the big guy with the laugh. He's got a slice and about a thirty-five handicap."

"Why're you playing with him then?"

"You kidding? He's loan officer at Birmingham Federal. Listen, I was thinking —" He paused to drink down half the tomato juice. "Since I'm going to Freeport the end of the week — I told you that, didn't I?"

"I don't think so, you might have."

"We've got some investors, a group, coming all the way from Japan, if you can believe it. All the islands over there, they're looking in the Bahamas. So — I thought why not fly down with Bo this evening, see your folks. They probably have some questions, how late he can stay out, all that."

"I've been on the phone with my mother practically every day this week," Mickey said.

"Also it'll give Bo and I a chance to talk," Frank said. "See if I can get a few things straightened out about his attitude."

Mickey watched him pour another ten-ounce glass of juice. Was he kidding or what? He looked terrible, as though he could use another five hours of sleep; but he kept busy, putting on his shoes now, trying to act as though he felt normal. In their fifteen years together, Frank had never admitted having a hangover.

"The flight's at 6:30," Mickey said.

"I know, I called and made a reservation." He glanced up at her. "Couple of days ago. I thought I told you."

He was rushing it at her. "Let me get it straight," Mickey said. "You'll drop Bo off, see my folks and what, hang around Lauderdale a few days before going to Freeport?"

"Either way. I can see your folks. Then, I can stop at the tennis camp on the way back, like Friday, and come home Saturday."

"So you'll be gone all week."

"Now you've got it," Frank said.

"Well, okay. Then I'll drive you to the airport?"

"No, I'll drive, leave the car there. It's a lot easier, in case I get in late." Frank finished his tomato juice, getting every drop. "I drive, Bo and I can talk in the car."

There were questions she wanted to ask; but he would tell her he didn't have time now; later. So she said, "Bo has a match at one, the Inter-club. Are you gonna watch it?"

"I'll see. It depends on what time I get finished. So —"

She raised her face for the kiss on the cheek and felt his hand slide down the tennis dress to pat her can.

"— I'm off."

"Your name's in the paper, Frank."

"Hey, really? The club championship?" Turning back to her, his eyes seemed almost bright.

"No, it's about kids playing tennis. Remember we talked to the girl, the reporter? At Orchard Lake."

"Oh." He picked up the paper, glanced at the page a moment and dropped it on the counter. "Good shot of Bo. What's it say, anything?"

"You can read it later."

"Yeah, save it. Well — I'm off." He always said, "I'm off."

Frank went out the door that led to the attached garage. The door closed behind him. Mickey waited. The door opened again and Frank was looking in at her, frowning, scowling.

"What in the hell you do to your car, for Christ sake?"

3

Sunday, a nice sunny day, Ordell Robbie and Louis Gara were out for a ride in Ordell's tan Ford van. It was mostly tan. What made it stylish was the black-yellow-red stripe of paint worn low around the van's boxy hips. The tan van for the tan man, Ordell said.

He had not seen his friend Louis Gara in almost three years. Louis had been down in Huntsville, Texas, keeping fit, clearing scrub all day, having his supper at five P.M. and turning the light out at ten. Louis was back home and Ordell was showing him the latest sights of the Motor Capital. Things like the Renaissance Center on the riverfront, all that glass and steel rising up 700 feet in a five-tower complex.

Louis said, "Wow." He said, "It's big."

Ordell squinted at him. "That's all you can say? It's big?"

"It's really big," Louis said. "If it fell over you could walk across it to Canada."

"Take you farther than that," Ordell said. What he saw, looking up at the Plaza Hotel tower and the outside elevator tubes, the sun hitting on it hot and shiny, it looked like a gigantic spaceship could take you to the moon for about a buck seventy-five. Louis and Ordell had been smoking grass, too, lounged in the van's swivel captain's chairs, some Oliver Nelson electronic funk washing over them from four speakers as they drove around looking at the sights, working north from the river.

Six years ago Louis had been tapping a swizzle stick at Watts' Club Mozambique, messing up Groove Holmes' beat for Ordell who happened to be sitting next to Louis at the horseshoe bar. Ordell had put his hand with the jade ring on Louis' wrist and said, "My man, we don't go to your clubs and fuck with the beat, do we?"

Louis was high that time and feeling love for mankind, so he didn't take Ordell and beat him up the side of his head. He put the swizzle stick down and let Ordell introduce him to Campari and soda and they discovered what a small world it was. Unbelievable. Both of them had been in Southern Ohio Correctional at the same time. No shit — for true? But wait — and both of them had been in there for grand theft auto, supplying new Sevilles and Continentals to body shops and cutting plants down near Columbus.

They even looked somewhat alike, considering Ordell Robbie was a male Negro, 31, and Louis Gara was a male Caucasian, 34. Ordell was light-skinned and Louis was dark-skinned and that put them about even in shade. Ordell had a semi-full round afro, trimmed beard and bandit mustache. Louis had the mustache, and his head was working on a black curly natural, growing it out again after his time at Huntsville. Both were about six feet and stringy looking, weighing in around 160. Ordell wore gold-frame Spectra-Shades; he liked sunglasses and beads and rings. Louis wore a cap — this summer a faded tan cap — straight and low over his eyes. Louis didn't go in for jewelry; a watch was enough, a $1,200 Benrus he'd picked up at the Flamingo Motor Hotel, McAllen, Texas.

Ask ten girls which one they thought was better looking. It was close, but Louis would probably win six-to-four.

Woodward Avenue didn't look any different to Louis, the same bars, the same storefronts with grillwork over the show windows, a few more boarded up. It was a strange deserted big-city downtown with everybody staying out in their neighborhoods.

"Crime," Ordell said. "People afraid to come downtown; but there's no crime here. You see any crime in the streets?"

"Only the way you're driving," Louis said. "You're gonna get stopped for loitering."

"Coleman's got to fix this city up," Ordell said and sounded concerned, sitting low in his swivel seat, creeping the van along Woodward. Louis had to look over at him. Ordell said, "They build all the glass shit and convention centers and domes along the river? That's for the postcard pictures — hey, shit, look at Detroit, man — if you never seen it before. Then you drive out this big wide street, what do you see? What does anybody want to come here for? Pick up some ribs and leave the motor running."

"Over at the Mexican Village," Louis said, "on the wall in the can it says, 'Coleman is a copsacker.' Now you want a safe place and some good burritos, go the Mexican Village. All the cops eat there."

"I notice that," Ordell said. "The cops love to eat Mex. I was in there, it's right over by Michigan Central where I been doing some business."

"By the freight yards," Louis said.

"Freight yards, the Ho Chi Min Trail, man, all the stuff that comes out of there."

"That's where you're getting the building supplies?"

"No, the choo-choo comes in, we get mostly appliances," Ordell said. "Ranges, refrigerators, the man buys for these apartments I'm gonna show you. The building stuff we pick up out on jobs."

"This deal," Louis said, "if we're talking about lifting work you don't want me, you want some strong young boys."

"I say anything about lifting work?" Ordell looked at the rear-view mirror and made a sweeping left turn off Woodward. "I'll show you where the man makes his money."

Ordell made a couple of loops through the Cass Corridor area, giving Louis the tour.

"On the right you have the beautiful Wayne State University campus —"

"I had it two years," Louis said. "I should've learned something."

"On down the street," Ordell said, "to a fine example of neo-ghetto. I went to school too, man. You can see it's not your classic ghetto yet; not quite ratty or rotten enough, but it's coming. Over there on the left, first whore of the day. Out for her vitamin C. And there's some more — hot pants with a little ass hanging out, showing the goods."

"How come colored girls," Louis said, "their asses are so high?"

"You don't know that?" Ordell glanced at him. "Same way as the camel."

Louis said, "For humping, uh?"

"No, man, for going without food and water when there was a famine, they stored up what they need in their ass."

Louis didn't know if Ordell was putting him on or not. He looked at him, then shifted his gaze to the street again as Ordell said, "Uh-oh, see those people picketing? Trying to keep the neighborhood from falling in the trash can."

The van coasted past the people on the sidewalk, white and black, some with children, who were marching in a circle that extended from a bar to the entrance of an upstairs hotel. Louis read a sign that said, PROSTITUTES AND PIMPS GO AWAY. Another one said, HONK YOUR HORN IF YOU SUPPORT US.

Ordell beeped a couple of times and waved. A prostitute in white boots and hot pants waved back. There were prostitutes standing around watching, making comments, and a blue-and-white Detroit police cruiser parked at the curb. Most of the signs, Louis noticed, said, SEE AND TELL.

Ordell said he liked the one, GO HOME TO YOUR WIFE. He said, "If she was any good, the man wouldn't come down here."

Louis didn't understand the SEE AND TELL signs or the license numbers, it looked like, painted on a couple of other signs.

"That's the Johns' numbers," Ordell said. "Man stops his car to pick up a whore they write it down. Then the TV news man comes and takes pictures and the John's license number appears on the six o'clock news. How'd you like that, you're sitting home with mama and the kids? 'Hey dad, ain't that our car license?' Everybody's protesting. The other day I see these two ugly chicks look like pull-out guards with the Lions. I mean ugly, got these little halter outfits on, their tits hanging way down, they're walking along with a sign says, *'Lesbians Are Good Mothers.'* One's got this little kid. She's holding his hand, he's trying to get away to kick some beer cans. The little kid not knowing shit what he's into."

"Well, I've seen whores," Louis said. "What else you got, some muggings?"

"The whores're part of what I want to show you," Ordell said. "Be cool, Louis. You ain't got to be anywhere but with me."

He showed Louis where you could buy liquor with food stamps. He showed him the second best place in town to buy fine grass.

Finally he showed Louis the apartment buildings, about ten of them scattered around on different streets in the Corridor, all of them big, worn-out-looking buildings, four and five stories, with names like *Clairmont* and *Balmoral* and *Carrolton* chiseled in stone above the entrance ways. Louis said, yeah? They didn't look any different than all the rest of the ratty looking places. Jesus, Louis said, how could people live around here? Louis hated dirt. He didn't hate real dirt, soil. He hated manufactured dirt, soot, and all the wrappers and empty bottles and crap in the doorways. Why didn't the people who lived there bend over and pick up the crap?

"It's inside the apartments are different," Ordell said. "These the ones the man bought and fixed up. I'll show you."

He took Louis past an old Airstream house-trailer that was parked in front of an apartment house. The trailer was painted yellow with DYNAMIC IMPROVEMENT COMPANY lettered on the side, and in a smaller, fancy script, *Licensed Builders.*

"That's the man's company," Ordell said. "Dynamic."

"You're gonna tell me," Louis said, "he got rich renovating apartments?"

"He got rich buying the apartments cheap, then improving them even cheaper with materials and appliances and what have you supplied by the Ordell Robbie take-it-and-get, man, delivery company. You following me? He gets them all fixed up, then rents them — not to the po' black folks and the people on welfare and the ones got strip-mined and fucked over and come up here from the Kentucky hollers, shit no — he rents them to the pimps and the ladies with the high asses you like."

"So it's a business like any other business," Louis said. "What's the big deal?"

Ordell turned left off Third Avenue at Willis, pulled over to the curb and parked so he could swivel around in his captain's chair and look directly at Louis and see the whores in front of the Willis Show Bar.

"The deal — all these colorful people pay him in cash. You understand?"

"I guess they would," Louis said.

"Start multiplying," Ordell said. "He's got twelve buildings I know of, average thirty units each, two to $300 a month rent. That's a gross of almost 100 grand every month."

"And he's got taxes, overhead. You said he's buying buildings," Louis said.

Ordell gave Louis a pained look. "You think he uses his own money? He mortgages the buildings, ten per cent down. Yeah, he makes some payments. But he takes his rent receipts in cash, declaring only about sixty per cent occupancy. You listening? And he takes out around fifty grand every month, *fifty*, and goes and hides it."

"Where?"

Ordell grinned. "Gotcha, haven't I? He been doing this, we know of, two years."

"Where's the money?"

"In a bank."

"Well, for Christ sake, what good's that do us?"

"Bank's not in this country."

"So what? A bank's a bank." Louis stopped. "Wait a minute. He knows who you are, right? How you gonna work it?"

"He knows me, yeah, but just barely. One time I met him and a couple times maybe he's seen me. But I don't — shit, you think I deal with *him* and he buys the merchandise himself? Shit no. Listen, he don't even have his name in the company, not on any paper the company's got."

"You're talking about Dynamic."

"Yeah, Dynamic Improvement. You saw it. Man name of Ray Shelby runs it. He's the front for the man, been working for him years."

"Okay, he's putting money away —"

"And breaking the law, way he's doing it."

"Okay," Louis said, "you get next to the man and say excuse me, give me all your money or I start screaming and hollering. That's what you got in mind?"

Ordell shook his head, giving Louis a little grin. "Uh-unh, that ain't what I got in mind. Now I'm gonna take you some place else on the welcome home tour of the Motor City."

"Where we going?"

"Got to wait and see. This is a surprise mystery tour."

"Is it far?"

"About half hour."

"I better take a leak first," Louis said. He got out and crossed the sidewalk to the Willis Show Bar, the whores looking at his can in the tight pants and making comments.

Ordell was glad Louis was back from Texas. He liked Louis and liked working with him. They saw things the same and could bullshit each other with straight faces, not letting on, but each knowing he was being understood and appreciated.

When Louis came out he walked over to the van and looked in. He had an unlit cigarette in his mouth.

"Guy come out behind me?"

Ordell looked over past the whores to the Willis Show Bar entrance. "No — yeah, big guy?" Ordell, hunched down, could see the man now in the doorway. "Got on a Bosalini?"

"That's him. I'm in the can," Louis said, "he comes up, says hey, loan me some money. I say loan you some money? You need a buck for a drink, what? He says I want to borrow whatever you got in your wallet. Mother took $27."

Ordell was still looking past Louis toward the big black guy in the Borsalino felt worn straight on his head with the brim up and the high round crown undented.

"Go on out in the street and call him some names."

"I don't think it'd work," Louis said.

"Try it," Ordell said. "If it don't work, keep running."

"Gimme a match," Louis said. He was a little nervous.

Ordell watched him walk away from the van lighting his cigarette. Louis called out something to the big black guy and the whores looked over at him again. Now the big black guy said something, grinning, and the whores laughed and started juking around, feeling something about to happen. Ordell watched Louis begin to edge back now, throwing the cigarette away as the guy came toward him. Ordell heard Louis' words then, Louis calling the guy a tub of shit and, as the guy tried to come down on him, Louis faked a hook, feinting with it, and threw a jab hard into the guy's belly. Ordell put the van in *drive.* He watched Louis run past the windshield and then the big guy run past and make a cut and begin chasing Louis down the middle of Willis. Ordell brought the van out and started after them, creeping up on the big black guy who ran pretty well for a man his size. He had one hand up now holding his Borsalino on.

Ordell was looking down at him through the windshield when he beeped the horn. The big black guy jumped, trying to look around as he kept running, and Ordell punched him with the blunt front end of the van. Hit him and braked, seeing the guy get up and start running again, looking back big eyed. Ordell punched him again with the van, Ordell flinching, pulling back from the steering wheel, as he saw the guy's Borsalino crush against the windshield, right there in front of him. He jammed the brakes and the guy went down, disappeared. Louis came back and bent down, taking the guy's wallet, then throwing it aside and helping the guy over to the curb where he sat with a dumb dazed look on his face.

Ordell waited, watching Louis get in with the wad of bills folded in his hand.

"How much it cost him?"

"Couple hundred," Louis said. "I hope he learned something, but I doubt it."

4

Analyze it: why was it hard to talk to Bo? Because she was tense with him, guarded.

Why?

Because she was afraid to level with him.

Why?

Because she was always defending an untenable position. Playing make-believe, pretending everything was nice. So it wasn't Bo's fault at all, was it?

No, it was her own fault, always trying to be Nice Mom. Protecting him from what? Why in hell couldn't she be straight with him?

"Jeez, what'd you do to your car?"

"I guess I parked crooked. Your dad backed in —"

Bo waited.

"— and I guess my car was over too far in the center."

"He was smashed last night, wasn't he?"

"No, he wasn't *smashed.* That's an awful thing to say."

"I heard you. I mean I heard *him.* Did he throw something at you?"

"Of course not."

"How'd his trophy get broken?"

"It fell. He was putting it on the dresser and something was in the way. It fell off."

"How come he brought it upstairs?"

"I don't know, to look at it, I guess. He won the club championship — he's proud of it."

Silence. Mom and son in tennis clothes driving to the club twenty minutes before noon: Bo studying the strings of his Wilson racket, pressing the gut with the tips of his fingers; Mickey waiting for the lighter to pop, reaching for it and looking straight ahead at the road as she lit her cigarette.

"Where's your sweater?"

"I guess I left it out there."

"Are you sure?"

"I don't know. I guess so."

"You packed everything you'll need?" She knew he had; she'd checked his suitcase.

"I guess so."

"You're not going to have much time to get to the airport."

"I don't see why all of a sudden *he* has to go."

"Bo, how many times? You don't say *he*."

"You know who I mean."

"That's not the point." She stopped before adding something about respect.

"Okay, how come *dad's* going all of a sudden?"

"Because he has a meeting in Freeport next week and he thought —" What did he think? "— it would be nice if the two of you could fly down together. Give you a chance to talk."

Why did everything have to be nice? Like a TV family. Hi, mom. Where's dad? Dad's in the den smoking his pipe, wearing his old baggy sweater and working on your model airplane. Mmmmm, you making brownies, mom? Change the script and see what would happen. No, I'm smoking grass. What do you think I'm doing?

She wondered if Bo had ever smoked. She wondered what he was thinking right now. All she had to do was ask.

But she said, "Dad'll stop by Nana and Papa's with you and make sure —" What? "— you get settled all right. And I think he wants to call the tennis camp."

"I thought it was all set."

"It is. Just, you know, to make sure."

"He's gonna hang around and watch me?"

"No, I told you, he's going to Freeport."

"How about today? Is he gonna be there?"

"He'll try to. He's playing with a customer."

"I hope he doesn't come."

"Bo —" Now what do you say? "That isn't nice at all." The word again. "He loves to watch you."

"He loves to tell me what to do and he doesn't know shit."

"Bo!"

"Well? Does he?"

"He tries to help you."

"He does?"

"He's encouraging you, he wants you to win."

"How can he help me? He doesn't know a topspin volley from a groundstroke."

"He knows the basics. You don't have to be an expert to offer advice, do you?"

"If you say so, mom."

She waited and stopped herself from calling him "young man," and saying something traditionally altogether dumb. If he was right, why couldn't she agree with him?

She wanted to say something, desperately. But she held back. She tried it in her mind several times. She tried it again while she drew on the cigarette one last time and rolled the window down and threw out the butt.

"Bo —" she stopped.

"What?"

"When you come back — we don't have time now."

"For what?"

"A talk. As soon as you come back. Bo — let's cut out the baloney and tell each other how we really feel. All right?" She had rehearsed saying, "Let's cut out the bullshit," but couldn't do it.

Bo looked at her. He didn't seem surprised. He just looked up and said, "Okay."

She felt relieved, just a little self-conscious. "I think I understand how you feel. I mean about dad. Sometimes we let people bother us too much and we feel guilty when we really shouldn't."

"I don't feel guilty."

She was injecting her own problem. "I don't mean necessarily guilty. I mean we sometimes feel distressed, you know, disturbed, when there's no reason to. We sort of let things get out of hand."

She was using words instead of sticking to feelings and losing him.

Bo didn't say anything. Mickey was conscious of the silence. She wanted to fill it, quickly.

"Are you worried about your match?"

"Why should I be worried?"

"I mean have you been thinking about it, planning your strategy?"

"I played this kid before," Bo said. "He's big, he's almost sixteen. But he's got a piss-poor backhand."

"Well," Mom said, "you should beat him then. Right?"

Mickey waited for Frank in the main hall off the lobby. She wandered past the entrance to the grill, looking in, thinking the room was empty, and was trapped.

Tyra Taylor called out, "Hi, celebrity!" The three ladies in tennis dresses, at the table near the window, waved and motioned her to join them. "We were just talking about you. Come on and have a Bloody."

Celebrity. Tyra would hang onto that all day and use it to death. At least there were no other members in the grill. Mickey approached their table shielding her eyes with one hand, squinting, knowing Tyra by the annoying sound of her voice, but not able to see faces clearly with the wall of glass behind them and the sun reflecting off the lake. Tyra Taylor, Kay Lyons and Jan something, with three Bloody Marys and three empties, getting a good jump on Sunday. Tyra said she loved the article, it was darling. Jan agreed and told Mickey she should be proud. Mickey said thank you, not sure what she should be proud of. Kay asked her, straight-faced, what it was like being a tennis mom.

But Tyra was still saying the article was darling and the picture of Bo, Bo was darling, wasn't he darling? So Mickey didn't have to answer Kay.

She wrinkled her nose a little and said she didn't think much of the way it was written, though it was probably accurate as far as it went. (She wasn't trying to be cute with the nose wrinkle. Why was Kay looking at her like that?)

Kay said, "The girl wrote it straight, didn't she? The moms did the talking?"

"I guess what I'm saying, I thought it was loaded," Mickey said, "out of balance."

"What you're saying," Kay said, "you're not a real tennis mom and you wish the hell you hadn't been there."

Kay smiled — she was still a buddy — and Mickey was instantly relieved. Tyra could call her a celebrity and belabor the darling write-up and it wouldn't matter so much. At least someone knew she wasn't a tennis mom. If she had time, she wouldn't mind joining them, she liked them.

But sitting with the ladies — it was a strange thing — Mickey would be with them but not with them. She would be perched somewhere watching the group, herself in it — the same way she saw herself with Frank when they were arguing. Never completely involved. The ladies appeared to talk in turn, but they didn't. There was an overlapping of voices and topics changed abruptly. Mickey wondered if there was something wrong with her, why her attention span was so short when it came to cleaning ladies, cub scouts, the PTA, clothes, golf scores, tennis strokes, historical love novels written by women with three names, dieting, what their husbands liked for dinner, how much their husbands drank, how their husbands tried to make love on Saturday night and couldn't, face-lifts, boob-lifts, more dieting —

She would think, What am I doing here? Then think, But if I weren't here, where would I be?

She would try to think of something she would like to talk about. She would think and think and finally give up. (One time she had asked, "Do you know how people communicate with each other on the planet Margo?" But no one asked how, or even seemed to be listening. Barbara or someone was telling what her kids liked for breakfast.)

Mickey would watch and half listen, or let her mind wander, or find herself studying Tyra Taylor's perky moves, asking herself, Do I do that? Tyra was forty pounds overweight in a size 14 tennis dress. She would sit with her back arched, her head cocked pertly and nibble celery like a little girl. She was deceiving. Tyra appeared animated, but told long, boring stories in a nasal monotone about her maid's car trouble and her dog's hemorrhoids. Her dog, a miniature schnauzer, was named Ingrid. (Tyra would give Ingrid doggie treats saying, "Her's hungry, isn't her? Yes, her is, yes, her's a nice little girl," over and over, mesmerizing Mickey who didn't often speak to dogs. She was never sure what to say to them. She would think, Try it. But she couldn't.)

Mickey got away from the Bloody Mary ladies saying she had to see Frank and then get out there and be a tennis mom — ha, ha — but she'd have a drink with them on the porch later. She waited in the hallway a few minutes, watching the door that led to the men's grill and locker room, then came back into the main grill and sat at one of the near tables. When Rose appeared, Mickey asked her if Mr. Dawson had been eating lunch. Rose said no, he was in there having a beer. Rose said she told him his wife was in the big room and he said fine, he'd be right out. Mickey thanked her — she felt awkward — and said she might as well have an iced tea. She lit a cigarette and continued to wait . . . hearing Tyra's voice . . . nodding and saying hi to the members in tennis and golf clothes coming in for lunch.

They'd stop and act surprised to see her and ask what she was doing all by herself. What's the matter, was she anti-social or something? Didn't she have any friends? Mickey would smile or pretend to laugh and go through the story about Bo's match and waiting for Frank, just having a quick iced tea.

Why did she pretend to laugh? It was all right, everyone did. But why was she tired of it? If she felt like giving them a smart-ass answer, why didn't she?

Because she couldn't think of a smart-ass answer fast enough.

No, that wasn't it. It would be fun, though, if she had the nerve. They'd say, "How come you're all alone?" And she'd say, "Because I break wind a lot." Or they'd say, "How come you're all alone?" And she'd say, "Because shithead knows I'm here and he's making me wait."

Marshall Taylor said, "What're you thinking about?"

He squinted across the grill and waved to Tyra, then looked down at Mickey again with a solemn expression and winked. Marshall Taylor, with a Deep Run golf cap sitting on top of his head and golf gloves on both hands, winked, leaned in over the table and seemed about to tell her something confidential.

He said, "How are you?"

"I'm fine," Mickey said. "How're you, Marshall?"

He frowned as though in pain as he glanced over at the window. Maybe be didn't like Marshall; the name. Most of the members called him Marsh.

"I seem to recall saying something last night while we were dancing. You remember?"

Mickey remembered, but looked puzzled. "What?"

"I asked you if you'd have lunch with me."

"You were drinking — we all were, we say things —" showing him how pleasant and understanding she was. "Don't worry, I didn't take it seriously."

"But I *was.*" He stared at Mickey with a pretty straightforward, serious look too. "I meant it."

"Isn't Tyra waiting for you?"

"If she's watching we're talking about the piece in the paper. I haven't read it yet —"

"Don't."

"What I'm gonna do is cut out the picture, put it in my wallet."

"Marshall, come on —"

The name wasn't right. Marshall was too formal for a guy trying to fool around. But Marsh was too soft for a six-four hulk who'd played defensive end at Michigan State and now owned a company that made steel extrusions.

He said, "I mean it. I want you to have lunch with me."

"But there wouldn't be any point. I mean, why?"

"I like to talk to you."

"We talk. We're talking now."

"You remember any of the things I said last night? I told you how I've been thinking about you —"

He had told Mickey how different she was. He had told her, dancing — his hand moving over her back and trying to work in beneath her arm for a feel — she was like a little china doll. So much easier to dance with than Tyra. Dancing with Tyra was like driving a semi. She was putting on weight. Lived only for herself. Spent money like it was going out of style. Always buying clothes — but could never look as good as Mickey did in her simple little outfits. And — his wife didn't understand him. The club lovers actually said that. "My wife doesn't understand me." Mickey wondered if she was supposed to say, "Oh, then let's fool around. Frank doesn't understand me either." It was true, and maybe the club lovers didn't get along with their wives; but why did it mean she would want to have lunch with them? What happened to those guys on Saturday night? A few drinks and respectable family men, dads, became lecherous pains in the ass. At one time she had thought maybe she should drink more at club parties, join in and quit watching. Everyone seemed to be trying to get involved with someone else. But why get involved and pretend to have fun simply to pass the time? If she was bored —

A week ago Saturday evening, sitting in the cocktail lounge, opening up a little to Kay Lyons, Kay had said, "If the parties bore you, don't go."

Mickey: I don't mean I'm bored. It just seems like a waste of time, every weekend the same thing.

Kay: Then do something else.

Mickey: But if Frank likes to come — entertain customers, all that — it's what a wife does, isn't it?

Kay: What is?

Mickey: Be with her husband. Do what he wants to do.

Kay: Why?

Mickey: Because it's expected. He's —

Kay: The breadwinner: I don't know, I usually

come out alone. God knows where Charlie is most of the time.

Mickey: Then you choose to come here. You like it.

Kay: What else is there to do?

Marshall Taylor, leaning on the table with his golf cap sitting on top of his head, said, "You thinking about it?"

Mickey said, "Marshall, I have to go. Bo's got a match and I have to find Frank —"

"I understand he's going to the Bahamas," Marshall said.

"Just for a few days. An investors' meeting."

"I asked him if he wanted to play next Saturday, he said he'd be away."

Mickey hesitated, nodding. "Probably all week, but he isn't sure."

"How about tomorrow then for lunch? I know a good place — if you're worried about being seen."

"Tomorrow — no, I really can't."

"How about Tuesday then?"

"Really, it's not a good idea, Marshall." Her gaze moved past him, through the entrance to the hallway and the all-yellow outfit approaching. "Frank's coming." She didn't mean it that way, as a warning.

But Marshall winked at her and said, "I'll call you later." He turned to Dawson with a grin. "You leave your wife sitting alone, Frank, somebody's liable to steal her." He started away.

Frank turned on his grin, swiping at Marshall's shoulder. "See you out there, partner." Then turned off the grin, pulled a chair out and sat down.

"Well?"

"I saw you as we drove in," Mickey said, a nice even tone. "I thought you were starting at 9:30."

"Is that why you brought me out here?"

"If you weren't playing right away — I wanted to tell you Bo's match was changed to 2 o'clock."

"You send a waitress in to get me —"

"I asked Rose if she'd seen you."

"You send a waitress in to get me. She says, 'Your wife wants you.' Like that, like, 'So you better get out there.' "

"I didn't say it that way."

"Let me finish, okay?" He waited, in control. "You send her in to get me, I'm supposed to jump up and come running out, huh?"

"Frank, I didn't mean to interrupt you."

"I told you at home I'd watch Bo's match if we finished in time. You remember my saying that?"

"Yes, but then the time was changed and I was wondering about your flight."

"Don't worry about it."

"Well, if the flight's at 6:30 and you haven't gone out yet —"

"Don't *worry* about it, okay? We're going out at 1:30. Larry didn't get here, he was late. But I'll keep you posted, every move," Frank said. "Let's see, so far I've had two shells and I just ordered a cheeseburger and french fries. If I have another shell with lunch that'll be three, right? What do you think, you want to write it down or can you remember?"

"Frank, I'm sorry. I didn't mean to interrupt you. Why don't you go back in?"

"When we get through playing I'll probably have a couple more beers," Frank said. "Let's see, that'll be five. Six if we have one at the turnstand. Then a couple of drinks at home, a couple on the plane. That's, let's see, ten."

Mickey got up, taking her pack of cigarettes.

"A couple more with your folks," Frank said, "that'll be twelve —"

5

Richard Edgar Monk lived at 1035 State Fair, the street that ran east of Woodward Avenue along the south edge of the Michigan State Fairgrounds. The house faced a chain-link fence and was directly across from one of the gates where they used to bring in the horse-trailers during the racing season and Richard made eight dollars a day parking cars in his drive. But now they played softball over there.

The house was a frame crackerbox with a pair of dormer windows sticking out of the roof and no style at all until Richard fixed up the front with imitation ledgerock, a grillwork porch and striped aluminum awnings over the porch and windows. There was a hedge around the little square of grass to keep in the pair of flamingos, a bird-feeder on a pole in the backyard and a statue of the Blessed Virgin standing in a birdbath that Richard's mother had bought. Before she had died, Richard's mother used to go out there by the bird-bath and say her rosary for the conversion of Russia. She and Richard had both hated atheistic communism.

What had happened in the last eight months: First, Richard's wife, Dot had left him, taking four-year-old Richard Jr. with her. She had never complained or said a word about Richard's mother living with them; but according to the note that had been the reason she left. She couldn't stand it any longer, the woman telling her how to cook, where to put the dishes in the cupboard, how to toilet train Richard Jr. The note had not said much more than that. Then his mother had died of a heart attack a few months later at the age of sixty-seven. But there was no way of locating Dot to tell her. All he knew was Dot and Richard Jr. were somewhere in California, because he received postcards of Disneyland and orange groves about once a month, saying they were fine and the weather was hot but cool in the evening.

Richard wanted to go to California to look for his wife and boy and believed he could do it himself because of his interest in police work and procedures. He read books on it, watched police shows on TV and, until recently, had had a job with Alert Security Services — patrolling shopping centers, rich neighborhoods and construction projects — which Richard felt was good training. The trouble with the job, he'd only made three-sixty-five an hour, one-ten a week take-home, had to buy his own uniform and wasn't able to save anything. So he had begun drawing fifty bucks on the side to disappear or look the other way whenever the coon came at night in the truck to pick up building materials. That was fine until he got questioned, read-out and fired without notice.

Now he had a two-tone blue police uniform and no job. He was patiently waiting for the big one the coon, Ordell Robbie, told him was going to come any time now.

Ordell had said to Louis, "You ain't ever in your life seen anything like Richard Edgar Monk. Wait till he shows you his war room."

Louis wanted to say to Ordell, man, I don't believe it. The van was parked outside the cute house on State Fair that Sunday afternoon. They were inside visiting with Richard, upstairs now, letting Richard show them his gun collection and World War II memorabilia. Louis was a little confused at first.

He said, "Your dad was in the war, right?"

"Tank gunner," Richard said.

"Well, let me ask you," Louis said. "What side was he on?"

Richard looked at him straight, 240 pounds of Richard in his T-shirt and police pants with the light-blue stripe down the side, crew-cut head looking at Louis — no screwing around with Richard — not a glimmer of anything in his blue eyes.

"My dad was with the 9th Armored. KIA at Remagen, March 12, 1945. I was two years old."

Louis said, "Oh."

The reason he was confused, there were photographs of American soldiers sitting on tanks; but there was also a red, white and black swastika on the wall; pictures of German soldiers cut out of magazines; a photograph of Adolf Hitler, and a nice shot of Heinrich Himmler in his black SS uniform.

Ordell was watching Louis taking his time to look at all the stuff on the wall before he got to the gun display. Ordell said, "See, Richard says the Germans the best soldiers in the world and it don't matter about sides now. That right, Richard?"

Richard must have nodded. Louis didn't hear him say anything. Louis said, "How come they lost then?"

"Logistics," Richard said, "their troops divided up on two fronts. The way it should've been, we should've been over there helping them fight the Communists."

Jesus Christ, Louis thought. Again he said, "Oh," and picked up a copy of a tabloid newspaper with the name THUNDERBOLT on the masthead. Published, he noticed, by the National States Rights Party. Louis came to a poster and glanced over at Ordell. Ordell was grinning. The lettering on the poster said, *Nothing is lower than Niggers and Jews, except the Police who protect them.*

Ordell said, "Richard believes some niggers are all right though. Hey, Richard?"

"Some," Richard said.

"The rest he want to send back to Africa —"

"The ones on welfare," Richard said.

"Yeah, the ones on welfare he want to send back. I say, Richard, but Ah's from Cleveland. He says it's all right for me to stay. Least till we get this job done."

Louis reached the conference table that displayed Richard's arsenal, an assortment of rifles, revolvers, a musket, shotguns — one sawed off — several grenades, bayonets, trench knives, a gas mask, a German helmet, an Afrika Korps soft hat, Nazi armbands, belt buckles, an SS death's head insignia, boxes of cartridges and shotgun shells.

"Show him some," Ordell said.

Richard picked up the musket first. "Well, this here is your Kentucky rifle, black powder musket. That little sawed-off's a Mercury 12-gauge double barrel. Let's see, you got your Mauser, German K-43 semi-automatic . . . Beretta M-59 Assault Rifle, holds twenty rounds. Here's your famous Walther P.38, some people think is a Luger . . . your Colt .45. . . . your Smith and Wesson Combat Masterpiece . . . Iver Johnson Sidewinder, some Saturday night specials that ain't worth a shit for killing anybody, I mean stopping them, but they're sort of interesting, you know? Here's my favorite weapon, Colt Python .357 Mag. Son of a bitch weighs almost four pounds. It'll knock a man down and tear a hole in him big as a fist coming out."

Ordell said, "That the one you carry?"

"When I'm on duty," Richard said.

Louis said, "You ever shoot anybody?"

Richard looked at him and seemed to think about it before saying, "Not yet."

"Over here," Ordell said. "What's it called, Richard?"

"That's your Valtox drug-screening kit," Richard said. "Runs you fifty-nine ninety-five." He walked over to the open vinyl case, sitting on a wall shelf, that contained small bottles with eye-dropper tops and what looked like test tubes. "You can test over twenty-five different drugs. Marijuana, hashish, your amphetamines and opium alkaloids, also your LSD, STP and so on." Richard picked up one of the bottles. "This here is your new cocaine odor test. Put a drop on the material and if it's cocaine you get a smell like, it's like a wintergreen mint."

"Brush your teeth with it and get high," Ordell said. "What else you got?"

Richard's thick body revolved slowly as he looked around, raising stubby hands to rest on his hips. Like a guard in a concentration camp, Louis thought. Jesus.

Richard said, "Well —"

"You notice in the drive?" Ordell said to Louis. "He's got an AMC Hornet, man, pure black, no shit on the outside at all, your plain unmarked car. But inside — tell him, Richard."

Richard said, "Well, I got a rollbar. I got heavy-duty Gabriel Striders. I got a shotgun mount in front."

"He's got one of those flashers," Ordell said, "Kojak reaches out, puts up on his roof?"

"Super Fireball with a magnetic bottom. Let's see," Richard said, "I got a Federal PA one-seventy electronic siren, you can work it wail, yelp or hi-lo. Well, in the trunk I keep a Schermuly gas grenade gun, some other equipment. Night-chuk riot baton. An M-17 gas mask." He thought a moment. "I got a Legster leg holster. You ever see one?"

"He's gonna see everything," Ordell said. He took Louis into the hall, squeezing past Richard. He showed Louis the bathroom and opened the door to a small bedroom. "Big enough, huh?" Louis looked in. He saw a vanity made of blond wood and a single bed covered with a decorative chenille spread.

Downstairs, Ordell said, "Don't Richard keep a nice house?" He made a sweeping motion with his hand, presenting the lace curtains and furniture to Louis, the fat maroon couch and easychairs with crocheted antimacassars on the arms and head-rests. "He's a good cook, too," Ordell said. "Fixes noodles with about anything you can name. Don't you, Richard?"

"I like noodles," Richard said.

Ordell was picking up the Sunday *Free Press* from the coffee table, looking for a section. He said, "I'm gonna take a piece of this, Richard. Okay?"

No, Richard was shaking his head. "I haven't read it yet."

"I'll leave the funnies, man. I just want this part here."

Outside, getting into the van, Louis said, "Jesus Christ, I don't believe it."

"I told you he's beautiful," Ordell said. "I love Richard. Make a wonderful screw at some maximum security joint." He dropped the section of newspaper on Louis' lap and started the engine.

"See, what he does, Richard trips on that Nazi shit; makes him feel big. What I like about him, in his mind there ain't any bullshit. I mean everything's in order."

"His *mind,*" Louis said. "That guy's got fucking cement for brains."

Ordell glanced at the rear-view mirror pulling away from the house. "Sure he does, but that's the beauty. I tell him the man's a big rich Jew, that's all Richard has to hear. See, it's for the cause then. It's like you wind him up — he'd do it even if he didn't need the money so bad."

"What's he need money for, buy some more guns?" Louis glanced at the newspaper that said, across the top, FOR AND ABOUT WOMEN, and caught the word *tennis* below it.

"No, he needs to find his old lady. She ran out on him."

"Jesus, I don't blame her."

"Yeah," Ordell said, "first time in years his old lady is probably happy. Don't have to get up and salute the swastika."

Louis was holding the newspaper open now, looking at the full page of photographs of tennis moms and their kids.

"Which one is she?"

Ordell reached over and pointed to one of the pictures. "That one. See over near the end it's got something about, this man saying how much it cost him for his kid to play?"

"Yeah?"

"That's the man. Spend six, seven grand a

year on tennis balls."

Louis was still looking at the picture of Mickey Dawson.

"I was expecting her to be older," he said. "An older woman. You know, she's not bad looking in the picture."

"You're gonna see her for real," Ordell said, "if we can work it, get up close to the place."

"It says her name's Mickey."

"You hear what I said?"

"What place? This is some tour, you know it?"

"Out where the rich folks live," Ordell said. "Call' the Deep Run Country Club."

"I been there," Louis said. "I played golf there once."

6

Louis had been here about thirteen years ago, right after he got out of the Navy and was going to Wayne and the guy in his Introduction to Psychology class asked him if he ever played golf. He'd forgotten the guy's name — a first name that was like a last name, Stewart — that was it.

The place looked different now. The fairways on the right, driving in the winding road through the trees, that was the same; but he didn't remember all the tennis courts on the other side — about eight or ten of them, over there behind a wall of bright green windscreens. There seemed to be a lot of people over there. They heard a quick cheer and some clapping, not very loud.

Louis remembered he had shot about 120 and lost 13 of Stewart's golf balls, some he couldn't even find on the fairway. Stewart never invited him back. The prick. No, Stewart was all right. He wondered if he'd recognize Stewart if he saw him.

The clubhouse looked different too. Louis remembered a big white frame colonial looking building. He didn't remember the pillars by the entrance or the ivy growing all over the sides. Ordell made a circle around the entrance, past the young guys who parked cars — the young guys giving the van a look — and drove into the parking area along the side of the clubhouse away from the tennis courts. They could hear kids yelling, sounding as though they were playing in a swimming pool. Louis didn't remember a pool.

"How do you know?" Louis said.

"It was in the paper," Ordell said.

"I didn't see anything about it." Louis held up the women's section.

"Saturday paper. Tell about the different tournaments and the kid's name was in it." Ordell crept the van, looking for a parking place. "Everybody out at the club," he said. "Nice sunny day." He came to a stop at the end of the aisle, giving up. Louis looked at him.

"You can't park here."

"Go ahead. I'll wait for you."

They looked out past a chain-link fence at sailboats on the lake. There was the sound of an outboard, off somewhere. A Cadillac crept up behind them, then swung over to the next aisle.

Louis said, "You don't want to walk around over there, huh. People think you're the shoeshine boy come out for some air."

"I don't need to go," Ordell said, "I've seen her."

"Yeah," Louis said. "Let me borrow your sunglasses." He got out and walked through the lot and past the clubhouse toward the tennis courts.

The big fifteen-year-old kid had won the first set 7-5 and was on top of Bo Dawson 4-1 in the second, standing back and returning everything Bo hit at him, making Bo play the big kid's slow, steady game. Bo would run out of patience and jump on a shot to put it away and that's why he was losing.

That's what the people in the stands said who were watching the match in their tennis and golf outfits. They said somebody should talk to Bo, slow him down before he blew the match. Bo wasn't playing his usual game; he was off stride. Someone said Mickey was probably dying. Looks would pass between the people in the stands, eyes raised, a slow head-shake. Comments were made quietly because Bo's mother was sitting on the bottom row of the stands that were built along one side of the court. On the other side, beyond a second court, another crowd watched from a line of umbrella tables.

Someone said Bo wasn't stroking; he was too anxious and his timing was off.

Louis wanted to say the kid was concentrating on his acting instead of the match, going through a lot of tragic motions. He'd blow a shot and then strike a dramatic pose: look up at the sun — Why me, Lord? — or closely study the strings of his racket. A couple of times, when people were moving in and out of the stands, Bo looked over and glared and waited until the people were seated.

Something he learned watching TV, Louis

thought. Louis couldn't understand why tennis spectators were so polite. Why there had to be silence during a match. He'd think of a major league ballplayer in a tough situation: a batter with a three-two count waiting for the ball to come in at him ninety-five-miles-an-hour, and the fans screaming and banging seats. Louis wondered if he'd have to sit here the rest of the match. He didn't see how he'd get down without disturbing people.

He had a pretty good view of Mrs. Dawson, on an angle looking down, and could see her face when she turned to look at the right-hand court. When her son was over there she faced that way most of the time. She looked even younger than in the picture, not more than in her late twenties; but she had to be older to have a son Bo's age. She didn't look like a girl who got knocked up in second-year high and had to get married. She looked like a girl, a woman, who had money. What was it about a woman like that? Her hair maybe. It wasn't overdone in some bullshit hairdo like you saw on waitresses. Or the way she sat. She seemed at ease; though Louis could tell she was strung-out inside, nibbling there on her lower lip and smoking one cigarette after another.

Bo blew another one, an easy putaway. He tried to kill it. The ball cracked hard against the tape along the top edge of the net and dropped back into Bo's court. People in the stands said, "Awwww," and made sympathetic sounds as Bo let his racket fall and stood looking at the net with his hands on his hips.

Right, Louis thought, blame the fucking net. He noticed Bo's mother wasn't watching the act; she was lighting another cigarette. People were saying it was a tough break and, awwww, that was too bad, wasn't it? Louis liked the tall kid on the other side. The kid looked awkward, but he stood very calmly watching Bo. The kid was cool; he was content to let Bo beat himself.

Match point: Bo slammed one that sailed over the tall kid's head. The tall kid approached the net with a big grin, wiping his hand on his shirt getting ready to offer it. Bo turned around and threw his racket at the fence. He stood with his hands on his hips for awhile, people moving around now, crossing the court. Louis watched him. Finally Bo walked up to the net and gave the tall kid a brief handshake, not giving it much or saying anything. Bo's mother reached him as he was walking away, toward the umbrella tables, and put her hand on his shoulder and said something, no doubt sympathizing.

Why did everybody sympathize with him? Louis wondered. Why didn't somebody kick his ass?

Louis stood up in the stands, looking around. He noticed Bo's tennis racket still lying a few feet from the windscreen-covered fence, where it had bounced off. People walked past the racket going over to the umbrella tables and the other courts beyond, but nobody seemed to notice the racket lying there. Two couples walked out on the court, one of the men opening a can of balls. Louis stepped down the boards of the stands, walked over to the fence and picked up the racket. It was a Wilson Jack Kramer. He had picked up a Wilson at Palmer Park — it must have been twenty years ago — tried playing tennis, found out it was about a hundred times harder than it looked, and sold the racket to a kid for five bucks. This one was probably a much better racket. The strings were so tight he couldn't move them at all.

He'd say to Ordell, "Tennis anyone?" No, he wouldn't, he'd think of something else or let Ordell say something first. But Ordell would know he had a line ready and wouldn't ask him where he got it. So he'd throw the racket in the van and not say anything. The racket would stay there, in back by the rear speakers and the ice chest, on the red carpeting. Neither of them would say anything about it, though one or the other would pick it up from time to time and fool with it. See how long they could go, neither of them mentioning it. He liked to do things like that with Ordell.

Right now he'd like to find a men's room. He should've gone at Richard's house. Jesus, Richard was a spooky guy. Or wait till they went someplace to eat. Grass always made him hungry, the same as when he drank beer he was taking a leak every fifteen minutes after about the fourth one. He'd tell Ordell he had to go bad and Ordell would say, "What's the matter, you nervous?"

That's why Louis went into the clubhouse — to find a men's room — in the main entrance past the big colonial pillars. The time before, thirteen years ago, they had gone in a door that led directly to the men's locker room.

He hadn't been in the lobby before. He wondered if he'd see Stewart or recognize him if he did. There was a wide carpeted hallway. He saw people eating in a dining room with the sun on the window. He could hear voices, people laughing. People passed him in the hallway. He felt them looking at him and at the tennis racket, knowing he wasn't a member. All right, he was a guest. And the tennis racket was like any other Wilson Jack Kramer. He looked fine. No flashy print or colors, but the cap and sunglasses, nice lightblue sportshirt and tan flares were all right. He had almost put on jeans this morning at Ordell's apartment, but didn't because it was Sunday.

That was strange. Something left over. What was the difference, Sunday or any other day? Like Sunday was still the day of rest: get dressed and go to mass, have the big pork roast dinner at noon. That was a long time ago. Louis found a men's room in the hallway. He came out, recrossed the lobby to the main entrance, opened the door and stepped back as Mrs. Dawson was right in front of him, saying, "Oh, I'm sorry," hesitating. Louis moved aside, holding the door open with the tennis racket hand. She was really nice looking, right there close, moving past him.

Louis said, "Mrs. Dawson?" And watched her expression as she turned to look at him, expectant, a little surprised. Dark brown eyes.

"I think this is your son's racket. I found it out there, I was gonna hand it in at the desk."

It seemed to make sense, but he wasn't sure. She didn't question him. She took the racket, looking at it, and said, "Yes, it is. Thank you very much," still a little surprised. Her eyes raised with a very calm, pleasant look.

Louis wanted to say something else, hear her voice again, but he couldn't think of anything. He said, "That's okay," pushed through the door and got out of there.

In the van, sitting in his captain's chair, Ordell was sipping a can of beer, looking out at the sailboats. He swiveled around as Louis climbed in.

"You see her?"

"We had a nice chat," Louis said. "She said yeah, she'd love to spend some time with us."

7

Bo's explanation for losing: "That kid, all he did, he kept standing back at the baseline. What was I supposed to do, keep lobbing with him? It'd be like a couple of girls playing."

Mickey's explanation of why Frank was still at the club, drinking at several tables pushed together on the screened porch: "He has customers. He can't just rush off and leave them."

Bo said, "Well, isn't dad going? I thought he was so anxious."

"He said he'd call and get you, both of you, on a later flight."

Bo said he didn't want to take a later flight, get there in the middle of the night. He didn't even want to go. Why did he have to?

She wanted to say, "To learn how to play tennis. To learn how to lose without making excuses." She didn't though.

Bo said the whole thing, the tennis camp, was dad's idea. If he thought it was such a red hot idea why didn't he go to the camp? God, he could use it. Bo said he'd like to meet the kid again when the kid learned some tennis and knew how to play instead of dinking around.

They got home from the club at 5:15. Frank drove in at a quarter of eight, mad.

"All I said was" — very patiently, standing at her dresser, holding onto the edge with her elbow as she watched Frank pack — "at a quarter to five I said —"

"You said in front of everybody you were leaving."

"All I said was, I'm taking Bo home. The flight's at 6:30, you haven't packed and it takes an hour to get to the airport."

"Forty minutes."

He was packing now, moving between his dresser and the Gucci-striped suitcase open on the bed. She watched him drop in at least a half dozen dress shirts.

"All I said was —" He mimicked her, overdoing it. "I have to get Bo home and fix his dinner and clean the house and make some cookies —"

"I didn't say anything like that."

"Your tone, it's the same thing," Frank said. "Goody goody. Oh, isn't everything nice." He continued packing, laying resort clothes in the bag now, enough for at least two weeks.

Maybe she did use it a lot. *All I said was* — Mickey could hear the words. And maybe it was self-serving, playing nice, a cover-up for what she felt. But what was wrong with keeping the peace? Why antagonize people? Except she did antagonize

Frank, without trying too hard.

Okay, start over and get the tone right. She knew her thinking was fairly straight. It was just that she backed off whenever the chance came to express how she really felt, not wanting to offend. Or, wanting everybody to like her. But why couldn't she talk to her own husband?

Keep it harmless. "What time's the flight, eleven?"

"Eleven oh five."

"You sure you don't want me to drive you?"

He gave her a look: she was on dangerous ground again.

"That's right, you want to have a car out there," Mickey said. "And you'll be back . . . Saturday?"

"I said Saturday or Sunday. But it might be next week, if I stop and see Bo on the way back. He's gonna be gone a month."

It was in her mind to say, Why? You hardly ever see him when you're home. But Frank would come lashing back, or make it sound as though she was nagging him. Something was strange. This morning he'd said he was coming home Saturday, be gone a week. (Usually on his business trips to the Bahamas he was gone three or four days, at the most.) Now he was talking about staying, either in Freeport or Fort Lauderdale, until the following week. She tried to picture him, briefly, entertaining a busy, scurrying group of Japanese investors . . . then, standing in the sun, watching a bunch of kids at a tennis camp.

Mickey said, "I'd better call my mother, tell

her you're coming in later."

"Why don't you do that?" Frank said, the edge still there . . .

But gone without a trace only minutes later, mixing vodka and tonic at the kitchen counter, talking to Bo while Bo sat at the breakfast table with a bag of potato chips. "I'm sorry I didn't catch your match," the dad said. "That was a shame. I understand the guy wasn't too aggressive."

"*Aggres*sive, he played like a girl." Bo had sympathy and was pouting. "All he wanted to do was lob."

Mickey listened.

"He didn't have any backhand. He'd push at the ball, you know, like he was playing Ping-Pong, hit it up in the air with a little spin on it."

And Bo would break his back trying to kill it. Mickey stacked the breakfast and supper dishes in the dishwasher but didn't turn it on yet.

"The ball comes down, God, it'd hang there. You got so much time, you know, you want to kill it. What was I supposed to do, keep hitting lobs?"

Justifying, making excuses. He didn't get that from his mother. But then she wasn't sure.

Bo said, "If I played the way he wanted we would've looked like a couple of girls."

"I know what you mean," the dad said. "That's why I don't play mixed doubles anymore. It isn't worth it."

God help me, Mickey thought. She could beat Frank in straight sets and he knew it. But she didn't say anything. After a moment she began to wonder. Maybe he *didn't* know it.

The telephone rang while they were still in the kitchen. Frank, with a fresh drink and a plate of cheese and crackers, was sitting at the table with Bo. Mickey stepped over to the wall phone to answer.

Marshall Taylor's voice said, "Hi. Is this the Coast Guard? I was wondering if the coast is clear?"

Mickey said, "What?" She took another moment and said, "Oh, he's right here."

She listened to Frank say, "No, partner, I told you this morning I'm gonna be away. You remember now? . . . That's right. Yeah, Bo and I are leaving eleven oh five . . . You bet, partner. Shake it easy."

Coming away from the phone Frank said, "I think Marsh's getting hardening of the arteries."

Leave by ten they'd have plenty of time to make the flight, Frank said. He preferred to race to the airport rather than wait around at the gate with the amateur travelers who checked in a half hour or more ahead of time.

When they had finally gone, Mickey sat down at the breakfast table with a cup of coffee and her grocery list note pad. She wrote at the top of the page:

EXCUSES — JUSTIFICATION

She was thinking of Bo. Maybe he did get it from her.

No. She didn't make excuses. At least not out loud. She kept them to herself. What she did, when Frank annoyed her she would make harmless-sounding remarks she knew would irritate him — not often but often enough — then innocently cover up with, "All I said was —" She would jab lightly with the needle and then duck, instead of getting mad and letting him know how she felt.

Now then — In a stab at self-analysis she wrote:

Why don't you ever speak up to Frank when he (she almost wrote "pisses you off") — *does something you don't like?*

She began listing the reasons, adding her reactions to the reasons, her excuses, as she went along.

Because you shouldn't get mad.
(Says the goody-goody)

If you raise your voice, Frank raises his louder.
(An assumption, you've never raised yours)

Frank won't listen to you anyway. You're only his wife.
(Poor me. Meant to be funny (?)

Frank isn't aware enough to know there's a problem, a personality conflict.

(How could he if you keep it a secret?)

The final reason drew no reaction. There was no excuse for the excuse and it remained simply:

No guts.

Marshall called back at 11:30, the house quiet, Mickey upstairs getting ready for bed. He said, "*Now* is the coast clear?" The jerk.

She tried to sound a little annoyed. Don't call again, please. She had no intention of having lunch with him and that was that. Then said, "Let's not do anything dumb, okay?" Including herself in the game so he wouldn't be blamed entirely. Why couldn't she simply tell him to bag his ass?

"We'll talk about it. I mean we'll talk about us tomorrow," Marshall said. "I'll pick you up about one o'clock."

"I won't be here." Desperate. "I have to take my car in tomorrow."

"What's wrong with your car?"

"Oh — somebody ran into it."

"Let Frank take care of it," Marshall said. "Listen, the only time I can make it is around one. I'll call you first, give you the exact time. See, then I'll pull up in back, you run out and jump in. Right? Right. I'll see you." He hung up.

She wondered what it would be like if she did fool around a little, had an affair. Go to bed with someone else. If somehow it was all right.

Out of all the men at the club, which one would she pick?

Mickey thought about it, putting on her long pajama top, getting into bed, and reached a conclusion before turning out the light.

None of them.

At 3:30 the phone rang again. Mickey groped for it in the dark.

Her mother said, "Mickey?" making sure. Well, Bo arrived safely but hungry. She had given him a piece of homemade lemon pie and a glass of milk and finally marched him off to bed in the guest room that would be Bo's room for the next month, with his own bathroom, his towels and washcloth laid out, . . . and on and on and on, so Mickey was to relax and not worry about a thing. Mickey said that's fine, Mom. She said, "Are dad and Frank still up?" Her mother said, Frank? They wanted him to come home with them and offered to drive him back, but Frank said it was too much trouble. He was on the 7 o'clock shuttle to Freeport and insisted on staying at the airport. Said we'd just get home and have to come back. After a moment, Mickey said, "Well, you know Frank —" Her mother said, *Do* I. Frank and your father, those two would be up all night talking business. She said well, that's all she had to report. Mickey could sleep in peace now.

Mickey said, "Thanks, mom, g'night." And lay awake for at least an hour.

8

Ordell brought out his box of Halloween masks, set it on the coffee table in front of Louis and said, "Now you know how long I've been working on this deal."

They were in Ordell's apartment, Louis stretched out in a La-Z-Boy recliner with the Magic Ottoman up. He'd been sitting here four days on and off, since Ordell had met him at Detroit Metro and told Louis he was coming home with him. Louis had said home where? Some place in Niggerville? Ordell said no, man, nice integrated neighborhood. Ofays, Arabs, Chaldeans, a few colored folks. Ethnic, man. Eyetalian grocery, Armenian party store, Lebanese restaurant, a Greek Coney Island Red Hot where the whores had their coffee, a block of Adult Entertainment, 24-hour dirty movies, a club that locked the doors and showed you some bottomless go-go and a park where you could play 18 holes of golf. Does it excite you?

"I used to live there," Louis said. "Six Mile and Woodward."

"Live there again till you rich," Ordell said.

Louis had thought he should go to his sister's in Allen Park and take his chances on whether he and her husband Chuck would be swinging at each other by the second day. But once he stepped into Ordell's big four-bedroom apartment with a den, a dining room and a lady who came in to cook and clean anytime Ordell phoned her, well, this was the place.

Ordell had leased it a year ago when he was tight with a lady named Sandy and Sandy had invited two girlfriends to live with them who gave Ordell "rent money," twenty per cent of what they made entertaining tricks, so it wasn't like Ordell was pimping. They were cute ladies and the rent money they paid was usually twice as much as the $400 a month Ordell paid.

He liked it during the day, the cute ladies sitting around playing music, laughing at things he said. But he didn't care for the white Johns any, their attitude. Mostly it was a businessman who'd bring a customer to have a party and try grass and cocaine for the first time. (The ladies usually kept a couple of grams in the refrigerator. Ordell said he would not tolerate any scag though. He told them if he saw any lady in a scag nod he'd throw her ass out the window.) So Ordell would have these businessmen stumbling around in their skivvies sneezing, spilling drinks, shit, middle-aged jitterbugs trying to dance salsa with the cute ladies who'd be giggling, having some fun with them. Ordell said he knocked that shit off after four months and Sandy left with her girlfriends.

Ordell said he saw the man right here the first time. The man had brought somebody worked for a bank and bought them a $200 evening, about four hours worth of bullshit and a half hour in the bed. Ordell had found out the man was a big condominium developer-builder in the suburbs and, Sandy said Gigi said, he was also a property owner downtown. Property owner meaning a slum landlord, Ordell had thought at first.

"But no. Property owner meaning Dynamic Realty, which is the same almost as Dynamic Improvement Company," Ordell had said to Louis Sunday evening, driving home from the tour. "Now, you understand what I'm saying?" Louis had said, "Not all the way yet, but it's coming together."

So Louis had been sitting in the La-Z-Boy and getting up to eat, sitting there and getting up to go out and pick up a lady and get laid, twice — in between listening to Ordell tell him how they were going to make a million dollars and looking at the sights Ordell showed him. Louis did not get excited or ask many questions. He let Ordell make his presentation and dribble out things the way he wanted, taking his time. As Ordell said, "Be cool, Louis. You ain't got to be anywhere but with me." (For about six years, in high school and in the Navy and a little after that, Louis had been Lou; but Ordell always called him Louis. Ordell said, "Looo. That's not a name, man, that's a sound. Some places it's a toilet.")

Ordell and Louis had a good time looking at the masks.

Ordell had four Richard Nixon rubber faces; four because he originally believed it would require four people and he thought it would be funny if they were all Nixon and there was a witness wondering maybe if one of them was real. He and Louis put on Nixon faces for awhile and said, "Now I want to be perfectly clear on that," and tried to drink beer through the faces. Louis said yes, it would be funny, but who was gonna laugh, the cops?

Ordell had some horror masks he liked: rubber faces of different monsters, green and gray ones with big bug eyes and snaggled teeth. He had a Frankenstein monster mask he said was for Richard Edgar Monk. He had a good vampire face Louis liked, but it was too hot after a couple of minutes. They were all too hot, Louis said. Ordell said, here's a witch one. Here's, hey, some funny cartoon characters, Mickey Mouse and Donald Duck and Goofy.

Louis said they were too hot, you couldn't breathe in them. He said, "Don't you have any, you know, those little black masks, they just cover your eyes?"

Yeah, he had them. "I was thinking about for the lady," Ordell said, " 'stead of a blindfold, but we could wear 'em too."

Louis put on one of the small black masks and turned his head to look around, trying it out. Then Ordell put one on and they both began to grin.

This was the mask they'd use — no question about it now — the kind you always saw on crooks in cartoons and old comic strips: the guy with a mask and a cap like Louis' and a striped sweatshirt opening up the safe.

Ordell said he was also thinking — to wear instead of regular clothes? — these warm-up suits he saw at K-mart, fifteen bucks, blue with a yellow stripe down the pants. Louis stared at him and Ordell said, "No, huh?" Louis said no.

"Otherwise what do you think?" Ordell waited.

"Well," Louis said. "I don't see a schedule of events."

"It's loose, but it can go any time now. See, what we are, we're flexible," Ordell said.

Louis thought some more. "Where'd you say the bank is?"

"Freeport, Grand Bahama Island. Called the Providence Bank and Trust, in the Churchill Building."

"How do you know that's where his money is? Or it's still there?"

"Because of my good friend Mr. Walker," Ordell said, "who draws $300 a month from the account I opened when I went down. My friend Mr. Walker, a onetime bone-fisherman going big-time with a twenty-foot Boston Whaler and a '72 Vega imported from Miami. See, right away the gator in him come out and he began flashing. But it's cool, because Mr. Walker is right next to Lisabeth Cooper who works at the Providence Bank and Trust and has the second biggest pair of titties in the Bahamas on ladies twenty-five or younger. She keep Mr. Walker informed."

"Who has the biggest pair?" Louis said.

"Lady live out at Eight Mile Rock, also a close friend of his. Hey, you think the colud chicks here have high asses, wait, man."

"You must've spent some time there, doing your homework."

"I went there the first time — never told you? — it was, must've been seven-eight years ago. That was when I first met Cedric Walker, the bone-fisherman. I had this idea how to take off this entire hotel, every room in about twenty-five minutes, but we never done it."

"Why not?"

"I'll tell you about it sometime. What else you feel about this one?"

"Well —" Louis had to think. "We tell the man to switch the money from his account payable to your account. Then he's gonna know who you are, right?"

Ordell shook his head. "He only knows what my number is. They number accounts. We call the bank, find out it's been deposited. Then we write a check, transfer the whole thing to another number account in Nassau."

"*We?*" Louis said.

"That's right. I got a form you're gonna sign, make it a joint account."

"How'd you learn all this banking stuff?"

"Talking to people, man. It ain't hard. They understand you got money, you can do anything you want. Pay a little bit here and there, shit, it's easy."

"Okay," Louis said, "the guy's pulling about fifty grand a month out of Detroit, the apartments and whatnot, and banking it in the Bahamas for his retirement."

"Not declaring it, paying any taxes, any of that shit," Ordell said.

"Okay," Louis said, "why isn't that enough? Hold that over his head. He pays or you go to the Federal Building. I mean why do we have to complicate it with something they can call in the FBI for?"

"Because I *know* he's doing it," Ordell said, "but I can't prove it in the Federal Building. You think the man's dumb? I told you, there's no papers with his name on it. Ray Shelby is the president of Dynamic and there's *nothing* says the man is behind him and making all the money."

"How come he trusts Ray Shelby?"

"I don't know," Ordell said. "Maybe he's got pictures of Ray doing it with a donkey. What I think is, the man pays him enough, that's all. Ray's got a good deal."

"How come Ray tells you all this?"

"Ray doesn't know he's telling me. You squeeze out a little bit here and there and put it together. Peek in Ray's office, that house-trailer, when he's not there and look around. Ray was the man's construction super before the man set him up downtown, doing the apartments."

"Okay," Louis said, "we send the guy a note,

we call him or what?"

"We call him on the phone."

"He's not gonna like it." That was a dumb thing to say, but Louis was trying to think of everything at once and he was starting to think out loud. He said, "She never sees us, who we are."

"No, she don't see us. She got the mask on with tape over the eyeholes."

"How about — okay, let's say he's scared enough, he doesn't see any choice. He doesn't call the cops. He goes through with it, he pays."

"Yeah? That's the way it's supposed to work."

"What's his wife gonna think? How come he didn't call the cops, the FBI?"

Ordell frowned. "Because they get into it, it's his ass. They want to know how come he's got all that money in the Bahamas."

"I mean what if she doesn't know about it?" Louis said. "After, what does he tell her?"

"He tells her to hush her mouth." Ordell still looked puzzled. "What difference it make what he tells her? If she don't know, it's *his* problem."

"I mean after — what if she gets pissed off at him for not doing anything?"

The telephone rang. Louis glanced over at the desk sitting in the bay of windows.

Ordell got up, Halloween masks spilling from his lap. "Not *doing* anything? The man paid a million dollars to set her free, ain't he?" He walked over and picked up the phone.

There was something that bothered Louis, but he couldn't put his finger on it. He heard Ordell say, “Richard” — his voice bright and alive — “How you doing, man? . . . Yeah? . . . Yeah? You don’t tell me . . .”

Louis kept wondering if the man had told his wife about the money he was putting away and if it made any difference one way or the other. Yes, it was the man’s problem, but he kept wondering what could happen if the man’s wife got pissed-off at him. She could make an awful lot of trouble for the guy. Ordell had showed him their house, big English-looking place with the dark beams outside, set in concrete that had been stuccoed over. Ordell had also showed him the guy’s latest condominium project — about a hundred units going up and the sign saying

GRANDVIEW MANOR ESTATES

FAD Designed Homes
for as low as $39,995.00

“There’s a FAD in Your Future!”

Frank A. Dawson Associates

Louis had looked at it and said, “That’s a grand view, all right. Of Chrysler’s Mound Road assembly plant.

The guy, Dawson, had a lot to lose.

“Aw *right*,” Ordell said, coming away from the phone, clapping his hands together once. “That was Richard. Richard was out in his black Hornet doing his surveillance he calls it and says the man left the house at 10 P.M. with a suitcase, went out to Metro and got on a Delta flight to Fort Lauderdale, Florida. Like he does every month or so."

"Richard found all that out?" Louis sounded surprised.

"Richard'll fool you," Ordell said. "Only thing different this time, man had his boy with him and his boy had a suitcase. And you know something. That's even better. Leave mama home alone."

Louis said, "So you're thinking about tonight? Right now?"

"No, I want to call Mr. Walker first, see if he ain't drunk and his shoes are dry. Make sure of everything," Ordell said. "But I don't see nothing wrong with tomorrow."

9

"Give us about an hour," Ordell said to Richard on the phone. "We got to pick up something to use . . . Richard, we not gonna drive up in the van. We got to get something else, then make a switch. You understand? . . . Right, now see, what you do" — Ordell looked at his watch — "Richard, you better give us a little more than an hour. Say, call us at between eleven-thirty and quarter to twelve . . . Yeah, the number I gave you, the pay phone . . . Yeah, that's cool, Richard. We see you later."

Ordell looked over at Louis Gara having his morning coffee in his skivvies, his bare feet up on the coffee table where the box of masks was still sitting.

"She's out in Pontiac someplace at a bump shop, getting an estimate," Ordell said. "Second one she's been to."

"I was thinking maybe a Detroit Edison truck," Louis said, "or Michigan Bell. You know, look like we're making a service call."

"We don't want to keep it more than about a

half hour," Ordell said. "Come back, make the switch at the parking garage and leave it there. I mean whatever kind of vehicle you like. Sound good?"

"Fine," Louis said. "You've got it mapped out. I don't see we have any problems, long as you say Richard can handle his end."

"I programmed him, pushed the *on* button," Ordell said. "Now he moves till you shut him off."

Mickey was home before eleven with her estimates. Frank would call that evening and she would tell him — straight, without the needle — it would cost him somewhere between $5- and -$600 to have her car repaired. Which seemed unbelievable. She might as well play it straight, because Frank would play it down. So, it would cost him $100 deductible; don't worry about it. Don't worry — but what about the inconvenience? Getting the estimates ("Yeah? What else did you have to do?"), being without a car for awhile ("You can't get a ride to the club?"). Right, forget the whole thing. Frank was paying for it. Frank paid the bills. She rode along. (Her mother said, "Isn't he a wonderful provider? He's so good to you. You have everything you want.")

He would call in the evening and — maybe she wouldn't mention the car at all.

Marshall, the lover, would call around noon with, "Hi. The coast still clear?" Or some dumb thing. She could let the phone ring, not answer. Except it might be Bo. Or her mother about Bo.

Through the kitchen window over the sink, as she filled the tea kettle, Mickey saw the policeman in the backyard. He was walking across the grass from the drive toward the patio. Then he was over too far for her to see him. Mickey turned the water off and listened. After a moment she left the kitchen, moved through the back hall to the family room and stood looking at the French doors that opened onto the patio. The curtains were pulled back, panes of glass sparkled in the sunlight. She could see the wrought-iron patio table, the canvas chairs. There was no sign of a policeman. Mickey moved back through the hall to the kitchen and was approaching the door to the garage when the front-entrance chimes rang. She jumped.

The policeman was standing close, almost on top of her as she opened the door, the dark-blue uniform bulging at her, the serious, round face beneath the hat brim staring solemnly. He smelled of perspiration.

"Yes," Richard said, "we're investigating an alleged burglary in the neighborhood and I wonder did you hear or notice anything unusual last night or early this morning."

Mickey held the door open all the way, the air blowing the man's odor. She had to concentrate on what he was saying because the uniform distracted her. It was so busy. She wondered why the designer hadn't stopped before making the epaulets and pocket flaps and buttons light-blue. And the stripe down the pants. The badge said something, but she couldn't read it.

"No, I didn't hear a sound. Who was broken into?"

"Well, there was several houses," Richard said. "One of them didn't know it till we come around investigating."

"I'm sure no one came in here," Mickey said.

The policeman's eyes moved past hers. "You *are* sure. You checked the house?"

"I'd *know,*" Mickey said. "Wouldn't I? Everything was in order this morning. Nothing missing."

"You checked your basement?"

"No, I haven't been down there."

"Well, I noticed looking around outside," Richard said, "you know one of your basement windows is broken?"

It startled her. "No, I didn't. Are you sure?"

"Well, I can tell when a window's broke." Richard didn't smile; he meant it. He said, "You want me to, I'll come in and have a look around."

Mickey stepped aside. "Yes, please. I'd appreciate it."

He asked Mickey how to get downstairs. When she took him into the back hall and opened the door to the basement, he said she didn't have to go down with him, he'd find it all right. He was gone only a few minutes, came back up the steps filling the stairway — right hand pressed against the tooled-leather Tex Shoemaker holster that held the big Colt Python — then looked both ways along the short hall. Richard didn't say much when he was investigating. He went into the family room, crossed to the French doors and looked out, then jiggled the knob, trying to turn it.

"It's locked," Mickey said.

Richard drew the beige curtains closed, then reached in between them and jiggled the door knob again.

"How about your upstairs?"

"I know it's in order," Mickey said. "The basement's the only thing I wasn't sure of."

Richard didn't volunteer information about the basement. He said, "I wonder if I could use your phone."

Mickey brought him into the kitchen, Richard glancing at a card palmed in his hand. As he dialed a number Mickey asked him if he'd like coffee or iced tea.

Richard stopped. He said, "No thanks," then had to dial the number again. He waited, then straightened as he said, "Yeah, this is . . . uh-huh, I'm at —" He looked over at Mickey. "What's that address here?" She told him. "I'm at twenty-four twenty-two Covington. There's a broken window in the basement, but everything seems okay. There is no MO as at the alleged burglary. Doors all locked. The one in back by the patio would seem to be the way to get in, but I don't see it's been touched . . . That's correct. Yeah, well, I'll keep on then . . . Right." He hung up.

"Was there much stolen?" Mickey said.

"Where?"

"The houses that were broken into."

"Well, the usual. TV sets, jewelry."

She let him out the front door and waited to

watch the plain black car back out the drive and disappear up the street. She assumed he was with the Bloomfield Township Police. But why wasn't he driving a squad car, with the emblem on the side? She tried to remember what the local police cars looked like.

Louis had picked up a florist delivery van parked on the side of a gas station, the key in the ignition, waiting to be serviced or all through, Louis couldn't tell which. It ran all right and he drove it straight out Woodward ten miles to Birmingham and met Ordell and the tan van on the lower level of the town's south parking structure. They went up a flight of concrete steps to a vestibule and waited nearly twenty minutes for the phone to ring.

Ordell picked it up and said, "Richard, my man." He nodded most of the time, saying, "Uh-huh —" But hung up shaking his head. "Richard and his alleged."

Louis said, "She's home."

"She's home," Ordell said. "We go in through the patio."

Down on the lower level again, Ordell took a shopping bag out of the tan van and brought it over to the florist van. Louis waited behind the wheel. When Ordell was in he opened the shopping bag, brought out one of the black masks and handed it to Louis who put it in a side pocket of his blue nylon jacket. He was wearing his tan cap with it, and jeans.

Ordell brought the revolvers out then, both of them .38 Smith and Wessons, Detective Specials. He handed one to Louis.

"Just in case," Ordell said.

"I know," Louis said.

"I don't want to use it. I don't intend to," Ordell said. "But if somebody is standing between me and going to Jackson for forty years then it's too bad, cause I'll use it. You understand what I'm saying?"

"I know," Louis said. "It's not a choice."

Marshall Taylor spent the morning at Detroit Diesel discussing cold-form extrusions — sucker rod couplings, swage nipples, bull plugs — and looking at his watch. He tried to get out before eleven-thirty so he wouldn't have to take the purchasing guy to lunch. When he didn't make it, Marshall thought it over and made a decision with a certain risk involved, considering that Detroit Diesel was Taylor Industries' best customer. At ten to twelve — the purchasing guy having already assumed he was going to be taken somewhere for the martinis and the New York strip sirloin — Marshall said Jesus Christ, he just remembered a previous engagement, and exploded out of the purchasing guy's office. (Fuck him, he could eat in the cafeteria.)

All the way north on Telegraph to Bloomfield Hills, Marshall kept telling himself it was worth it. He decided he wouldn't stop and call Mickey, as he promised. (He'd call the purchasing guy later and invite him out to the club Saturday with his wife.) What he'd do, he'd get to Mickey's house about a half-hour early, hopefully while she was still getting dressed. He imagined her opening the back door with some kind of shorty housecoat on, just bra and panties on underneath. He'd say why didn't he make them a drink while she got dressed. Tell her to take her time. Then throw a couple of martinis together fast, run upstairs with them and catch her standing in the bedroom in the bra and panties, about to slip her dress on. They'd look at each other. He'd walk over. She'd let the dress fall to the floor —

Louis drove the florist delivery van past the house twice, 2422 Covington, the English-looking house. On the third pass he swung into the drive, brushed the high hedge and took the van all the way to the back. The garage opened on the back-yard side. Louis made a tight turn, a quick adjustment, and pulled in next to the Grand Prix. The woman might have heard them. She might have caught a flash of the van if she'd been looking out the window.

Ordell stepped around the van to the door that led inside the house from the garage. He tried the knob carefully. It didn't budge.

"Show time," Louis said. He took his cap off, snapped the black mask in place and put his cap back on. They looked at each other, maybe both of them thinking the same thing: something to tell later on: what they looked like standing in the garage with their Halloween masks on, fairly tense because it was about to happen, but both of them grinning a little. As though it had to be a little cuckoo or else it wouldn't be worth doing.

Maybe both of them thinking shit, what am I doing here?, as they ran low along the back of the house, underneath the windows to the patio. Ordell put a hand flat on the French door, turned the knob with the other and the door pushed in easily, then stopped against the curtains. That was no problem. They got into the family room and stood listening. Louis remembered the feeling now, what it was like to break into somebody's house. It had been a long time ago; even longer ago than the time he had played golf at the country club. Ordell was peeking into the hall, slipping the .38 Smith out of the hip pocket of his flared jeans. Louis put his hand in his jacket pocket, but didn't take the gun out. Ordell glanced back at him, motioning with his head.

They walked through the hall to the kitchen.

When Mickey turned the water off and came around from the sink with the dishtowel in her hand she jumped and made an odd sound, sucking in her breath.

Ordell said, "Trick or treat, mama."

Louis didn't waste time. He walked up to her, seeing her eyes widen, scared to death — the dark-brown eyes — turned her around and held her by the shoulders, not feeling her try to resist, as Ordell got out the mask for her that had tape covering the eyeholes. Ordell slipped it over her head, adjusted it just right, and Louis turned her to face him again. She seemed calm, her mouth slightly open. She had nice hair that was parted and slanted down across her forehead pulled and held tightly now by the elastic band of the mask. Ordell went over and opened the door to the garage.

Louis said, "She doesn't have any shoes on." She was wearing white slacks and a faded blue cotton shirt that looked to Louis like a cheap workshirt.

"She don't need shoes," Ordell said. "Come on."

Mickey said, "If you want money — my purse is on the breakfast table. I have some jewelry upstairs, not much —"

"Shhhh. Quiet," Ordell said.

They stood still, hearing the car then in the drive —the sound close to the house — then the idling, low hum of the engine in the backyard. Ordell stepped carefully to the alcove of windows by the breakfast table.

"Somebody — you expecting somebody?" He stared out, holding the beige curtain. "A man —"

Mickey couldn't think for a moment, in darkness, feeling the hands on her shoulders. "My husband said he was coming home —"

"Ain't your husband," Ordell said. He came away from the windows, motioning to Louis.

Marshall was surprised to see the garage door closed; even more surprised to find it locked. The outside kitchen door was also locked. So Marshall moved to the bay of windows and looked in, wanting to see Mickey but not wanting her to see him quite yet. She wasn't in the kitchen. But a purse was lying open on the breakfast table, and a wallet and ring of keys. He had to think.

If he went around and rang the bell — the obvious thing to do — there was a chance he'd be seen by one of the neighbors. He didn't know any of them; they didn't know him. But why risk it: start talk, maybe get Mickey in trouble. He was thinking of *her* — you bet he was — as he moved across the grass to the patio. The door would be locked and he'd have to knock anyway, ruining his chance of surprising her and having a little fun. It was the kind of thing she would like him for later. ("You big kook.") Okay, she was home. Probably upstairs now, changing.

Then another surprise: the patio door was open. In fact it was ajar, pushed in against the curtains. Okay, she'd been out in the backyard getting some sun — wanting to look good — saw what time it was and rushed in to get dressed. A little anxious maybe?

Marshall went through to the kitchen. There wasn't a sound in the house and he tried not to make any himself as he got the Beefeater and vermouth out of the cupboard below the counter . . . the ice, the lowball glasses . . . no olives; and he wasn't going to cut lemon twists. She was liable to come down any time and if he was going to surprise her — do something kooky — he might as well do it right. Marshall drank down half of a martini, refilled the glass with gin and gave it a swirl. There. He walked into the front hall and up the carpeted stairs with the drinks.

The next part would be tricky: surprise her without frightening her too much. He didn't want to catch her on the toilet either. His appearance was bound to give her a start. Then she'd be nervous, or pretend to be mad. He'd get her over that. He felt he knew how to handle Mickey. Gently. She didn't seem the type who liked rough stuff. She was giving, agreeable. He'd had the feeling for some time that Mickey was more than likely the type who couldn't say no. Whether because she liked it so much or because she didn't want to hurt your feelings, Marshall wasn't sure. But he was going to find out.

The open doorway at the end of the hall looked as though it led into the master bedroom. How about just, "Surprise!" But not too loud. Or — yeah — "Did someone say they wanted an ice-cold martini?" Dead-pan. Let her laugh first. Approaching the door he could see her sitting on the foot of the bed: her head lowered, as though she was looking down at her hands.

Entering the bedroom, getting his expression just right, Marshall said, "Did someone say they wanted —"

Her face raised as he spoke, something black covering her eyes. And something hard then nudging the side of his head. Wait a second — what's going on? He stepped back with one foot, careful of the drinks he was holding, turning to see what touched him. He caught a glimpse. He saw the revolver in his face and two figures, two masks, but not like Mickey's, there were eyes looking at him, one pair of eyes close, coming at him —

Ordell chopped Marshall across the head with the .38, grunting *unnnh* as he hit hard and pushed in against the man, inside the arms going out with the drinks, like a standup body block, jolting the man into the closet among the ten feet of hanging suits and cut him again, hard, across the head with the stub barrel, putting the man on the floor to sit wedged against the wall. Ordell shut the closet door and turned the key to lock it.

Louis was watching him.

Ordell shrugged. "I couldn't make up my mind."

"You did a pretty good job. Jesus, he's big."

"He's gonna have some blood on him, that's all."

Louis looked at the woman sitting rigid with her face raised like a blind person. He motioned Ordell into the hall and kept his voice low. "He's gonna wipe it off and call the cops. Soon as he gets out."

"It's what I'm saying," Ordell said. "We got to decide something."

Louis was trying to think. "He didn't see us."

"No, he didn't see much."

"We call Dawson tonight," Louis said, "tell him not to call the cops, this guy's already been there."

"I know all that," Ordell said.

"But we leave him dead," Louis said, "Dawson comes home and finds him, then Dawson — what's he gonna do with the guy? — *He's* got to call the cops then. I don't know, but I think we should quit talking and get out of here."

"Leave her?" Ordell said.

"No, take her," Louis said. "We're this far."

Not long ago in the men's grill they had been talking about clothes and one of the guys said, "Jesus Christ, Frank, how many suits've you got?" And Frank said, "I don't know. Couple dozen, I guess." Marshall Taylor remembered that.

Some of those suits were on the floor of the closet now, under him. Some had blood all over them. Marshall held soft cool silk to his head in the darkness, a sleeve. He didn't know what color it was. He wasn't sure what had happened. He was bleeding in darkness, his head throbbed like hell and he knew he was badly cut. His hair was sticking together in a hard crust.

There were no sounds; but that didn't mean anything. He lay quietly against the back wall of the closet to give his head a chance to stop bleeding and begin thinking.

Somebody had broken in. At least two guys. Mickey came home and surprised them. They tied her up — no, he wasn't sure about her hands. She was blindfolded though.

Did they actually have masks on? He wasn't sure now. They wouldn't hang around. They probably took some things and ran. Mickey would call the police —

They'd come up looking around and find him.

Take his name and address, see the martini glasses on the floor — ("We'd like to ask you a few questions, sir.") He had to get out of here.

If Mickey had heard his voice and if they were gone, she'd let him out before calling the police. Unless she was too frightened at the time and wasn't listening. He had only said a few words. Something about martinis. All right, if she didn't know he was here, where the hell was she?

Marshall looked at the luminous dial of his watch. He had been here a good fifteen minutes, not moving, his body cramped, stiffening. He had to do something. He could have stayed at Diesel. He could be at the Squire's Table right now talking about golf and cold-form extrusions, ordering the New York strip. Tyra would be out at the club.

Marshall kicked at the door with his heel, jarring his head and was afraid it would begin bleeding again. He lay still, waiting, telling himself he had to get out of here. Mickey wasn't home. He kicked at the forty-year-old door panel again and kept kicking, holding the raw silk to his head, his long leg pumping, smashing the wood, until the panel splintered and he was able to reach through and up and unlock the door. The martini glasses were on the floor. He went into the bathroom, looked at himself in the mirror, at the blood all over him, and felt panic again, hard, rigid fear. He washed some of the blood from his face. There was nothing he could do about his suit. Or about Frank's suits. He had to get out, but he didn't want to go downstairs. In the hall he stood listening for several minutes. He thought, A drink. God, that's what he needed, and that's what got him downstairs to the kitchen.

Mickey's purse was gone. The wallet and car keys were still on the table. The door to the garage was open. He could see Mickey's Grand Prix. Marshall pulled a bottle of J&B from the cabinet and had half a lowball glass of it, straight.

Okay. Say they had hit Mickey too. She hadn't heard his voice. She was dazed. She called a friend, somebody, a neighbor, to take her to the hospital. That's why she hadn't called the police right away. Go to Beaumont Emergency, that's where she'd be.

A head laceration could leave a lot of blood. All the blood in the closet — she'd tell the police yes, it must be hers. She was dazed, knocked out for awhile. They would assume it was her blood. No reason to check the type.

Marshall had another Scotch. That would be it; he'd have to be careful in case he was in some sort of mild shock. But he felt pretty good in spite of everything. Mickey'd go to Beaumont. He'd go to St. Joe's in Pontiac.

Questions then. How did it happen? He hit a tree. Or a light pole. His brakes didn't work. Where?

No. Some guy sideswiped him. Where? On Deep Run, right off Telegraph. He was on his way to the club; had a golf date with a customer. The guy sideswiped him, put him in the ditch and kept going.

Did he report the accident? Report it? He couldn't *see.* Christ, he had blood all over him, didn't he?

Marshall took a shovel from the Dawson garage. On the way to Pontiac he turned off Woodward into a deserted side road, got out with the shovel and, swinging it like a baseball bat, smashed in the left-front headlights and fender of his Cadillac DeVille, threw the shovel into the high brush and continued on to St. Joseph Mercy Hospital.

"Did somebody say they wanted —"

Wanted what?

She remembered the words and the sound of Marshall's voice because she had been waiting in silence, knowing it was coming, *some*thing, though expecting to hear him call out from downstairs first.

She remembered the awful sounds then. Grunts, hitting, the sound of Marshall's voice again choked off. She remembered one of them saying, "I couldn't make up my mind," and something else. The voices were fainter then, away from her.

Then close again, another voice, the white voice, saying, "Bring that." And the other voice saying, "You kidding?" A white voice and a black voice. A glimpse, in the kitchen, of a white man and a black man, though there was not that much difference in their color. Masks. A cap. The other one with a beard.

They took her by the arm, helped her into a truck or something. She thought of a funeral parlor, a hearse, with the heavy odor of flowers. She had to lie on the hard floor, on cardboard, feeling the bumps and jolts go through her, feeling to see if Marshall was with her and trying to brace herself. They didn't tie her hands. They didn't bring Marshall.

The black voice had said, "I couldn't make up my mind."

About what? Before that, just before that, a door had closed, a lock turned. Which would have to be the closet. They didn't know what to do with Marshall, couldn't make up their minds; so they had left him there.

Marshall would get out — if he wasn't hurt. Just some blood on him, one of them said. He'd get out and call the police. Look for two men in a — Marshall came after they did, so he would have seen the truck or whatever it was —

Going down a ramp now, into some kind of an enclosed place.

They opened the door. She was helped out and into another truck, feeling carpeting beneath her bare feet . . . placed in a contoured, cushioned chair, music suddenly blaring out next to her. She didn't hear their voices during the ride, only the music. Instrumental jazz. It reminded her of WJZZ-FM and some of the music seemed familiar. They were on a busy street. Woodward? Unless they were going east and west, across one of the mile roads.

The police would be sending out a description —

She wasn't sure of time; maybe a half hour had passed since they left her house, until the truck turned off the busy street. In less than a minute it made another turn and came to a stop.

When she was taken out, a hand holding her arm firmly, the white voice said, "There's a step. Then three more."

She was in a house that smelled old, but not musty. It was a kitchen smell, old grease, and it reminded her of something from the past. She was in a small house. Through the kitchen, a short hall, to a stairway: fourteen steps to the top, a cold bare floor, a hall, then into a carpeted room. She bumped against a bed and put her hand out to feel it, a bedspread with a deep-pile border or design.

Others were in the room, close, bumping things. She smelled stale sweat she had not smelled before. Someone else besides the black one and the white one was in the room. She turned her head and smelled cologne; no, a softer scent, a sachet. She was in a woman's room and again a memory stirred, something from the past.

The white voice said, "When you hear the door close, you can take off the mask."

"Where am I?"

"No talking allowed," the black voice said. "When you have to go pee-pee knock on the door and put your mask on."

She heard them moving again, the floor creaking beneath their weight. None of them touched her or said anything else. The door closed and there was silence.

After a moment Mickey raised the mask from her eyes.

10

Ordell had said, "For sure, he's a creepy guy. Lives here by hisself; nobody bothers him, wants to come near him. Can you think of a better place?" No, Louis couldn't. But he wished they were some place else.

Richard was standing in the doorway to the hall, looking into the living room at them. He said, "You want me to take the first watch?"

"Yeah, you take the first watch, Richard," Ordell said. "Hey, Richard —" He pulled the Frankenstein Monster mask out of the shopping bag on the floor by his chair and threw it over. "Put that on, man, you go in there. Or she comes out to go the toilet." He said to Louis, when Richard left, "I believe it's a good place. Can you think of a better one?"

"I told you, it's fine," Louis said. "What would he go in the room for?"

"It's his house," Ordell said.

"He doesn't have anything to say to her. What would he go in there for?"

"I mean if he happen to be face to face with

her," Ordell said. "That's all I meant. I'm not saying for him to go in there and do anything he wants. That what you thinking about?"

"We don't have any reason to hurt her," Louis said, backing off a little.

Ordell seemed to grin — Louis wasn't sure — looking over at Louis sitting on the couch with the parts of the newspaper spread out next to him. "No, we don't have to hurt her none. She gonna be up there by herself prob'ly a few days. Maybe she get bored, want a little something to do. You see Richard making it with her?"

I'd like to see his wife," Louis said. "I can't see Richard making it if he paid for it. No, what I'm saying, we get her upset — we got enough to handle without her going whacko on us. You don't know what a person, they get upset's liable to do. You keep the person reasonably scared, yeah, but you keep the person quiet, man, easy to manage."

"You don't want nothing to happen to the lady," Ordell said.

"Why should I? Do you? She's pretty cool about it so far, you know? You want to make problems we don't have?"

"I haven't said nothing. Man, I'm with you," Ordell said. "We're in this deal partners, man. Richard works for *us*. He does what we tell him."

Louis was going to say, Yeah, but just before you said, It's his house. Like he can do whatever he wants. But he didn't say it. He kept quiet now, deciding to wait and see. Whatever you were into, it didn't always work the way it was supposed to or the way the other guy said it would. You could have an understanding, thinking you both saw it exactly the same, and later on the other guy would say, "What're you talking about? I didn't say that. When did I say that?" Ordell said how it was going to work, what each of them, including Richard, was supposed to do; okay, he'd take Ordell's word for it. Otherwise he'd be worrying about things that might never happen. The way to play it, just don't be surprised if the other guy did something that wasn't in the agreement, because it wasn't a written contract or the kind of agreement you could point to and take the other guy to court and sue his ass over. You had to get along. It was good when two of the guys were close and there was a third guy they trusted but didn't give a shit about; it strengthened the closeness and lessened the chance of the two close guys fucking each other over; though it wasn't a guarantee. You did not want to be alone in something like this, naturally, it was too fucking scary. But if it meant saving your own ass — as Ordell had said, "If there's somebody standing between me and forty years in Jackson —" And Louis had said, "I know. It's not a choice."

That morning, Monday, Ordell had called his friend Cedric Walker in Freeport, Grand Bahama, and gave him Richard's phone number. Mr. Walker had called back collect: yes, the man had arrived on the early flight from Fort Lauderdale. He'd see what he could find out.

In the late afternoon, Mr. Walker called again. Yes, the man was on the island. No, a boy wasn't with him, he came alone. He hadn't gone to the bank, but Lisabeth Cooper was watching for him if he did. The man was at Fairway Manor where he had an apartment and always stayed and looked to be entertaining his lady friend who lived over in Lucaya. Ordell said what lady friend? He sat listening to Mr. Walker on the phone while Louis went out to the kitchen for a couple more bottles of O'Keefe Lager.

When Louis came back in, Ordell had hung up but was still sitting in the straight chair by the telephone table fooling with his beard. Louis handed him a bottle on his way to the couch. The end of the couch by the lamp with the cellophane-covered shade and the Little Bo-Peep base looked like it was going to be Louis' seat. It was the first place he had sat down in Richard's living room and, for some reason, he kept going back to it, looking at the lamp sometimes when they weren't talking and wondering what the Nazi was doing with Little Bo-Peep. There was something wrong with the guy. His wife or his mother probably had bought the lamp or won it across the street at the State Fair, throwing balls at wooden milk bottles, but there was still something wrong with the guy.

Ordell moved over to one of the deep maroon chairs, still thinking.

Louis said, "You gonna tell me or keep it to yourself?"

"The man's there," Ordell said, "staying at this apartment he's got on a golf course."

"Yeah, what else?"

"He got a lady with him. See, I knew he like the ladies, but I didn't know it was this same lady he's been seeing all the time when he goes there. I thought he had all kinds of ladies. Mr. Walker say no, it's the same one, good-looking young woman name Melody . . . Mel something . . . *Mel*anie. That's it, he say Melanie. Young foxy-looking chick; Mr. Walker say she lays by the swimming pool without her top on, these gentlemen come chipping onto number seventeen, that's right by the place, like the front yard. Man, they looking over there at Melanie, waiting for her to turn over, they lucky to five-putt the hole."

"That's an interesting story," Louis said. "What's the rest?"

"She don't work that Mr. Walker knows of," Ordell said. "But Lisabeth Cooper say she got four thousand seven hundred and two dollars in the Providence Bank and Trust."

"Say she's been saving her money," Louis said.

"Say shit. She spends it in the casino, but she's always got some in the bank."

"I don't see the problem," Louis said. "So the man's got something on the side."

"I don't say it's a problem," Ordell said. "But I like to know all the shit that's going on. I don't like surprises, man. I like to know, what's he doing there? What's she doing? Who is she? You understand what I'm saying?"

"Why don't you call him and ask him?" Louis said. He studied the clean, streamlined O'Keefe label. He liked the old one better. The new one gave him the feeling the beer was weak, watery. He said, "Why don't we call him? I'm serious. Get it done."

"Ask him about the foxy chick?" Ordell didn't see it yet.

"No, I mean tell him the deal. Why do you have to wait till he gets back?"

He could see Ordell hadn't thought about it, the possibility. Maybe there were some other things he hadn't thought about.

Ordell said, "I don't have his number." Now he was stalling, giving himself time to think.

"Call information. Or get it from Mr. Walker," Louis said. "The man's right there. All he's got to do is go to the bank."

Ordell was frowning, thinking hard. "See, he comes home, he finds out she ain't there. He *knows* something's happened to her."

"He calls home tonight," Louis said. "No, hey — we let her talk to him on the phone. "Honey, these men — I've been kidnapped —" Louis stopped, realizing something. It was the first time he had said the word or had even thought the word and heard it in his mind. Kidnap. Christ, they had kidnapped a woman. It wasn't simple extortion, leaning on the man, prying money out of somebody who was making it illegally and cheating the government, they had kidnapped the man's wife. Ordell hadn't used the word either. Talking it over it was always about the man, how they were going to jive the man into giving them a million dollars. Pay off Richard, pay off a few people in the Bahamas, they'd split, say, $960,000. You believe it? $480,000 apiece and the man couldn't say anything about it, couldn't call the police, couldn't do *any*thing. See, always the man. The man thinking he was so smart. They were gonna skin the man. And to make him jump right now and not get in a long conversation and give him time to lie or confuse them or move the money someplace else, they'd tell the man he'd never see his wife again unless he did what he was told. Nothing about kidnapping.

"Say call him, let his wife tell him," Ordell said, thinking about it. "He makes the transfer tomorrow. I call the bank, see the money was deposited —"

"We drop the lady home —" Louis said.

Ordell's gaze came alive and flicked at Louis. "With the police waiting."

"Okay, we put her on a bus."

"The police still waiting, wanting to know who put the man in the closet. Man with about fifteen stitches in his head."

"What she gonna tell them," Louis said, "she was kidnapped?" Christ, he said it again. "She doesn't know anything, because if she gets her husband involved they start asking him questions — all that money, huh? — dig into his business, his books. Before she knows it he's in Lewisburg, man, conspiring to defraud the United States government."

"Hey, it's interesting," Ordell said. "You know it? He's down there with the foxy chick his wife don't know nothing about. His wife's up here sitting on Richard's mother's bed, he thinks she's home making cookies. Yeah, it's interesting."

The Sony TV Richard had won and kept in the bedroom was now in this room. It sat on the vanity that had round corners and was made of lacquered blond wood, the back of the set reflecting in three panels of mirrors. She thought of Frank and his golf trophy. Because the vanity reminded her of the 1930s and the Empire State Building.

Mickey remembered snapshots of her mother taken in the '30s . . . her mother and her mother's two younger sisters, her grandmother . . . looking at the album every summer in the house at Gratiot Beach, the home on Lake Huron they called "the cottage" where there had been a vanity like this one in her grandmother's room. She remembered the sachet odor from that time, looking at her grandmother's "things," linens and silks (what were they, scarves, tablecloths?) folded in tissue paper and stored in a fat leather trunk, a treasure chest in an upstairs room where a pair of dormer windows looked out past a sweep of lawn to the beach and the lake that was like an ocean.

The dormer windows in this room were covered with a sheet of plywood, nailed tight to the frame with headless nails. In case she might try to rip the board off with her fingernails and jump out the window. Mickey had no idea where she was: within a half hour of Birmingham or Bloomfield Village, but in which direction? In a small, two-story house, blind behind the plywood to what might be a familiar view outside. Though she doubted it.

The little ruffle-shade lamp — the only light in the room except for a fixture in the ceiling — could be her grandmother's, but not the chenille bedspread with the peacock design in blue, purple and red. There was a print on the wall of a blond Christ Child, a scrubbed, well-behaved looking boy. The Sony, she noticed, was plugged in. They were considerate — a white man and a black man and a third one who had body odor, God, who stunk. Someone else recently had had b.o. A lot of people did. Why didn't they smell themselves? She'd have it too if they kept her in here very long. It was warm in the room. She had a nearly flat package of cigarettes, a lighter. Knock if she had to pee and put her mask on. It would be something to do. She wondered if they'd talk to her. Maybe they had the wrong person. Who was being kidnapped these days? People in Italy who had money. And the kidnappers got away with it. What was the last one here, in this country? A girl in a box underground who breathed through a tube. No, a more recent one. A woman tied to a tree in the woods, found after a couple of days. Both of them found alive, she was quite sure, and the kidnappers arrested.

Why would anybody — if you were going to kidnap somebody, why not pick . . . she'd never had her picture in the paper. Oh God, yes she did. But they couldn't have seen it and then planned it so fast. They must've seen Frank's name. *Frank A. Dawson Homes, Grandview Estates.* But even then, what did they cost? Grandview Estates wasn't money. What about the really wealthy people in Detroit? Somebody must've made a mistake.

God, kidnapped —

She couldn't believe it. She'd turn on the 6 o'clock news and there it would be. *Friend of family describes wife's . . . mother's abduction.* Friend of family.

Prominent industrialist trying to fool around with and get in the pants of friend's wife describes daylight abduction. Husband away on business not immediately notified.

When would they get in touch with him?

Local and county police have begun a thorough investigation . . .

The one who came to the door had smelled of perspiration. The policeman in the two-tone blue uniform, in the unmarked car. The same one, here.

It was planned. Of course it was planned. They had been watching her, waiting for the right time. And Marshall, the big jerk, had strolled in and gotten whacked on the head.

It was 10 to 5. The earliest news was on Channel 4 at 5:30. She was dying to hear how the friend of the family would explain what he was doing in the house between 12:30 and 1 o'clock in the afternoon.

"I just happened to be driving by and saw something suspicious," said Marshall Taylor, president of Taylor Industries, five-handicap golfer and country club lover.

Mickey sat down on the bed. A little self-analysis. How did she feel about all this?

Surprisingly, she felt fine. She felt — what else? Excited. More than that. Afraid? Yes, she was afraid. But she wasn't scared to death or petrified. Just the opposite, she felt alive. She was excited but calm. She had time to take what was happening to her and study it. She could perch up there wherever she perched and look at the whole scene, calmly watch what was going on and direct herself if she wanted to — yes, exactly — and give herself lines and use them. Say what she wanted. She didn't have to worry about a nice mom image. No points for nice moms here. She could be herself.

That was interesting. Mickey looked over at the triple mirror, at her reflection in the large center panel. She said, "Who are you?" She studied herself and said, "If you don't know, you're gonna find out, aren't you?"

She liked the feeling, being excited and calm at the same time.

11

Saturday, two days before they brought her, Richard had drilled holes in the doors at eye level and hung little framed silhouettes over the holes: a girl on the bathroom door and a boy on the bedroom door. He could move aside the silhouette, hung on a nail, press his eye to the hole that wasn't any bigger than a shirt button and see fine into either room.

The trouble was, the woman only had the clothes she was wearing, so there was no reason for her to take them off. There was nothing else for her to put on unless — Richard was thinking — he offered her one of his mother's nightgowns or a robe. All his mother's stuff was still in the drawers and closet and that might be a way to catch the woman naked.

Richard pressed his eye against the bedroom peep-hole and watched her pacing around, folding her arms and unfolding them, looking at things. She'd sit on the bed and then get up and pace some more and then sit in the rocking chair and rock fast at first, then slow it down and would seem calm. She was usually pretty calm. He wondered why she didn't turn on the TV. Richard would say to himself, Come on, take off your clothes and let's see what you got. He pretended he was inspecting a woman for breeding purposes. He'd look her over and decide if he wanted her to have his kid or not.

Maybe if it got hot enough in there she'd strip. Once, she reached in her shirt and scratched her left tit and adjusted her bra. That was as good as the show got, so far. He wondered why she never had to go pee. Maybe if he gave her a pitcher of ice water —

Finally, a little after five o'clock, she came toward the door. Richard moved the silhouette over the peep hole and stepped back. There was a knock on the door. Richard said, "Yeah?"

"I want to go to the bathroom."

Hot dog, Richard thought. He said, "You got your mask?"

"Oh —" Then after a moment, "Yes, I've got it."

"Put it on."

"How'm I gonna . . . do what I have to do if I can't see?"

"I'll help you." Richard grinned.

"Forget it."

"Just till you get in the bathroom." Silence. "You still want to go?"

"Yes, please. Open the door."

"Wait a minute." Shit, Richard had to get *his* mask. He came out of the war room wearing the rubber Frankenstein Monster face, his white T-shirt and his uniform pants. He wanted her to see him, but didn't know how he was going to work it. The monster face, the coon, Ordell, said was just in case. Like if she pulled her mask off.

She had it on, standing there waiting. She pulled back a little when Richard took her by the arm, then went with him the three steps to the bathroom. Richard said, "Here you go. When the door's closed you can take your mask off and do your business."

"Thanks," the woman said, not sounding as though she meant it.

Richard moved the girl silhouette aside and pressed his monster face to the peep hole. Now maybe he'd see something.

She looked at herself in the mirror first. Then ran the water and washed her face and hands, Richard thinking, Do that after. She was looking in the mirror again, running a finger over her front teeth. Come on, Richard urged. She turned to the toilet. Now. Undid her belt and the top button of the slacks, unzipped the fly. Right now. Pushed her panties down with her slacks and sat down all in one motion, her shirttail dropping down, covering her and, shit, all Richard got to see was a flash of her left bum. Goddarn it, her secret thing, her little nest right there and the goddarn shirttail was in the way. She was peeing now, he could hear her, then reaching around to flush the toilet —

Louis said, "What in the hell you doing?"

Richard got the silhouette in place as he turned and faced Louis in his monster mask. Louis squinted at him, then brushed past him to the door, lifted the silhouette aside and pressed his face close to the door. When he turned to Richard he said, "Jesus Christ —"

Richard said, "It's my house, ain't it?"

Mickey could hear them on the other side of the door — not words but voices, kept low. The one who smelled had brought her in here. Now one of the others was with him. She stepped close to the door about to press her ear to the panel to listen, and saw the drilled hole — freshly drilled, particles of unpainted wood sticking out from the round edge close to her eye. But she couldn't see through the hole. And she couldn't hear them now. There were footsteps on the stairs, going down.

When she knocked and the one who smelled let her out, taking her arm again, she returned obediently, in silence, to the bedroom, entered, heard the door close and took off her mask.

There was a hole in the bedroom door.

She saw it and looked away, walked over to the Sony and turned it on. Mike Douglas was talking to someone. What was his name? Always wore the dark T-shirt, long hair combed back — Carlson. George Carlin. She liked him. Frank had said, Who? He'd never heard of him. She sat on the bed and went through her purse, feeling the one who smelled watching her. The heavy policeman in the funny uniform. Except he wasn't funny.

This wasn't funny. Now what was she feeling?

She was mad. She was mad as hell. The fat smelly son of a bitch. She remembered Peter Finch, the nutty newscaster in the movie, in his raincoat. "I'm mad as hell and I'm not going to take it any more." She groped inside her purse, feeling for something long and thin with a pointed tip — like a knitting needle — but knowing she carried nothing long and thin. Lipstick An eyeliner brush. No pencil, not even for eyebrows. A cigarette.

There were four cigarettes left in the pack of True greens. She said to herself, Don't think. Light it.

She stood up, walked over to the Sony, switched to Channel 2 — to a police car moving, just what she needed — and back to 4. She snapped her lighter and lit the cigarette, moved back to the bed, lingered, moved past the bed to the closet, then to the blond dresser against the front wall, next to the door. He wouldn't be able to see her now.

Mickey reached out, inching the cigarette along the door panel, brought it almost to the hole and stopped. Then inched it again, close — and jabbed into the hole, losing part of the burning ember but feeling the cigarette go in cleanly and hearing, instantly, the scream on the other side of the door. Surprise, pain — Mickey wasn't sure. She moved close to the hole, withdrawing the broken cigarette, and said, "How do you like that, officer? You want to look in my basement?"

Almost at once she thought, You shouldn't have said that.

But it was done. She ripped the black tape from one of the eyes in the mask and pressed it over the peephole.

"This guy, I don't know, he thinks he's in the fucking Gestapo or something," Louis said, "looking through the hole when she's in there. Guy watches her take a leak."

"Yeah, maybe he's playing that," Ordell said. "Or see, Richard ain't getting much, he prob'ly forgot what a pussy look like. Wanted to refresh his memory."

"There's something wrong with him," Louis said.

"Sure there is," Ordell said. "His head got turned around or something or his mama dropped him out the window when he was a little baby."

"She probably threw him out when he tried to rape her," Louis said.

"Naw, he's harmless. He got all that shit up there, all the guns, but it's all he's playing pretend, thinking he's a big Nazi motherfucker, but it all stays there in his head," Ordell said.

Yeah, well they could beat it to death, they were stuck with the guy. Forget it. Louis said, "When you stop home, remember to bring some tapes."

"I will."

"The Lonnie Liston Smith. You know what he's got here, his records? He's got Rosetta Tharpe."

"He likes gospel," Ordell said.

"He's got James Cleveland. He's got Rosie Wallace, man, and the First Church of Love Choir.

If we're gonna be here awhile — You get the phone number yet?"

"I'm still waiting on Mr. Walker." Ordell was looking at Richard's big RCA black-and-white TV that was a piece of furniture with a pink and white bucking bronco statuette on it. "Here it is," Ordell said. "News is on." He sat up in the maroon chair and leaned on his knees. Then sat back again. They were anxious, both of them, but didn't want to show it.

There was a wreck on the Lodge Freeway. A tank truck had jackknifed and exploded. The driver had been rushed to the Ann Arbor Burn Center and northbound traffic had been backed up for hours.

There was something about a farmer having to shoot his dairy herd because of PBB poisoning . . . and pregnant mothers being interviewed, worrying about their milk . . . something on about PBB every evening but neither Louis nor Ordell knew what it was.

The sports editor, trying to sound like W.C. Fields, said the Tigers gave the Sox the Bird Sunday, Fidrych holding the Beantowners to five scattered hits.

Louis said, "Why don't they just say it, without all that cute shit?"

Sonny Eliot jumped around his weather map with his magic marker and his snappy weather reports. "High of ninety tomorrow, that's as welcome as a blowtorch in a firecracker factory, and no relief in sight." They waited through it in silence.

Coming up after about eight commercials would be Channel 4's latest crime report. Louis thought, Here we go. He noticed Ordell sitting forward again.

There was a quick run-through of current crime headlines with brief stories: Teens rob, shoot disabled freeway driver, proclaim, "We own the city" . . . Two stand trial in death of bartender . . . Witnesses finger more teen gang leaders . . . Gunmen shoot up Boys Home, staffer fired . . . Mayor Coleman Young says press too critical . . .

Louis seemed puzzled. "What's all this with the kids?"

Now a TV reporter with a swirly hairdo was interviewing members of a teen-aged gang, the Errol Flynns. Louis saw a bunch of skinny black kids standing around in their fifty-dollar Borsalinos like cowboys, grinning at the camera. Ordell grinned with them, saying look at them little Earl Flynns, hey, bullshittin' the man. Gonna eat him up. There were interviews with black neighborhood residents who said the police had to start hooking the kids up and throwing them in the clink . . .

In the *clink?* Louis thought.

. . . so the other kids would see them doing hard time and quit taking off the grocery stores and the old people's social security money so they could buy those Bosalinis and support their scag jones.

Louis said, "What's he talking about?"

"It's cool," Ordell said. "Listen to the man."

"Why don't they get to it?" Louis said.

There were more commercials, a preview of the top national and international news stories, but no more crime. Nothing about a suburban woman being kidnapped or abducted. Nothing about two dudes in Halloween masks breaking into a Bloomfield Village home. Nothing about a big dude holding two martinis getting hit in the head.

Ordell said, "You think the man's still in the closet?"

"You hit him," Louis said.

"I didn't hit him that hard."

"You hope you didn't."

They watched TV commercials and didn't say anything for at least two minutes, until the world news was coming on with John Chancellor.

Louis said, "I think somebody better get in his sporty uniform and go out there and investigate an alleged assault with the intent to put a guy to sleep and hope to Christ it hasn't turned out to be murder."

12

"What is it?" Mickey asked.

"Chicken and noodles cooked in chicken soup with onions and some other things, a biscuit in it. You'll see a biscuit in there but I don't think it'll kill you," Louis said, standing in the doorway with the tray. "You got your mask on? I can't tell."

"Yes."

"Okay, you can turn around. It doesn't matter."

Mickey turned and saw him through the uncovered eye in the mask: the white one with dark curly hair and a mustache in the shaft of light from the hall. Mickey stood on the side of the bed away from the door in shadow.

"Where do you want it?"

"I don't care."

"I'll put it on the bed."

She watched him place the tray near the edge, draw his hands away, then move the tray with its bowl of chicken and noodles and mug of coffee toward the middle of the spread, on top of the peacock's fanned filigree tail. He straightened and looked at her. He stared, then began to shake his head. He said, "Aw, come on —" and walked around the bed to where she was standing to touch the mask with the tips of his fingers. He pulled the mask off, up over her head, turning her around with his other hand on her shoulder.

"I used the tape to cover the hole in the door," Mickey said. "You'll have to get your kicks some other way."

"Yeah, well, you don't have to worry about that. We'll cover the holes."

"What's the matter with him? Why doesn't he bathe?"

"I'll ask him."

"He smells."

"He's got a few problems, but who hasn't, right? Eat your dinner," Louis said. "You want something else, knock on the door."

"What's gonna happen to me?"

"We'll talk about it after."

Louis took the mask with him to fix the eye hole. Jesus, it was a dumb idea. What're you doing? I'm fixing this Halloween mask. The whole thing — what're you doing here anyway? Answer that. But there was always a time like this when you thought it was going to blow up. Then it passed. Usually it did.

Richard had walked out nodding, rubbing his eye, not asking any questions. He walked back in exactly an hour and a half later still rubbing it. He said, "You know what that puss did to my eye?"

"Tell us about the other, Richard," Ordell said.

"Well, what I did," Richard said, shoving his policeman's hat to the back of his head, "I made sure there was no surveillance first. I cruised the street and the street back of the residence, the residence being dark, not any light on, but which didn't mean anything."

Jesus Christ, Louis thought.

"So then I went to a pay phone in the Kroger's, the corner of Maple and Lahser" — he pronounced it "Lasher" — and phoned the residence letting it ring twenty-five times."

"Twenty-five times," Ordell said.

"There being no answer I returned to the residence and pulled into the backyard and turned the car around before getting out. Then — I want to ask you. You leave the garage door open?"

"Yes, we did, Richard," Ordell said.

"The door from the garage into the house?"

"For Christ sake get to the alleged guy," Louis said, "will you?"

"Let him tell it," Ordell said. "Go on, Richard."

"Well, I went in —"

He went up to the bedroom like they'd told him, found the two glasses on the floor, the closet door with a big hole in it like it'd been kicked out from the inside . . .

Louis felt himself begin to relax a little.

. . . and the closet all messed up, blood on the clothes that were on the floor, but nobody in there. So evidently the witness had left.

"And not with any help," Louis said. "He kicked his way out. He was strong and healthy enough to kick a hole in the door."

Ordell sat back in his maroon chair. He was relieved, too, and could think now without a heavy unknown hanging over him, though there was still the big question.

"Why didn't the man go to the police?"

"I don't know," Louis said, "but I got a theory."

Louis had his mask on this time as he eased open the bedroom door a few inches. He said, "Mickey?" It was the first time he had used her name.

She didn't answer immediately.

"What?"

"Turn the light out and sit on the other side of the bed facing the windows."

"There aren't any windows."

"Yeah, well, where they used to be." He waited. When the light went off he opened the door wide and stepped inside. She seemed small sitting there, her shoulders hunched a little. He walked around the bed, out of the light into the darkened half of the room, and nudged her shoulder to hand her the taped mask.

"Here, I fixed it for you. Put it on."

Mickey took it from him and slipped the elastic band over her head as Louis sat down in the rocker facing her — two people sitting in a dark bedroom with masks on.

She said, "This is unbelievable."

"Yeah, I know. It's a little strange," Louis said. "If somebody walked in and saw us, huh? Well —" He sat back and began to rock. The rocker squeaked and he stopped.

"You watch the news?"

"Yes."

"Nothing about you on the 5:30 or the 6," Louis said. "How come?"

"What're you asking me for?"

"You have something going with that guy?"

"What guy?"

"Come on, the big guy walked in."

"He's a friend of the family."

"A friend, huh? Comes in the bedroom with the martinis —"

"He's a *friend.*"

"Then how come he didn't call the cops?"

"How do you know he isn't dead or in a coma?" Mickey straightened, her blind gaze facing the sound of Louis' voice. "You hit him with something, didn't you?"

"We checked," Louis said. "He let himself out."

There was silence.

Mickey said, "How do you know he *didn't* call the police?"

"Because the magic eye of television would've had it."

"Not something that happened this afternoon," Mickey said. "There wasn't time."

"So we'll see if it's on the 11 o'clock," Louis said. "But I don't think it will be. What do you think?"

There was silence again.

"You don't think so either," Louis said. "The guy, this good friend of the family, it doesn't look like he wants to get involved. You have a nice little thing going there, it's kind of exciting. Quiet bedroom in the afternoon, hubby's off building houses — As long as you don't get caught, huh? What's the guy gonna say?" Louis paused.

"Are you asking me?" Mickey said.

"No, I'm saying the guy looks around, he says hey, wait a minute. What am I doing here? Something's going on, it's none of my business."

"That's what he says?"

"I don't know him. I don't know what he's got to lose," Louis said. "What kind of a guy is he?" She didn't answer him. "Okay, put yourself in his place. You know him pretty well —"

"Nothing *happened*," Mickey said. "There wasn't anything going on between us."

"Hey, I'm not your husband," Louis said. "I don't care if you're screwing the guy out of his mind every Monday at twelve-thirty. But is he the kind of guy'd stick his neck out for you?"

Louis waited for her. He was sure she had tightened up inside. He felt the same way and it wasn't going to get them anywhere. He thought, Jesus Christ, and pulled his mask off. He felt a little better — watching her in silence, sitting with her hands in her lap — and wanted to help her. He didn't know how, but he did. It wasn't something to think about. He reached over, hunching forward in the rocker, hearing it squeak, and touched her face. She drew back. But he had hold of her mask and lifted it from her face as she pulled away from him.

Louis said, "What's he willing to do for you? That's all we're talking about."

Mickey looked at the figure hunched in the rocking chair, leaning toward her with his arms on his knees, waiting patiently.

She said, "I'll tell you something. I honestly don't know."

Tyra's ass looked as though it had been hit by Double-O buckshot at a distance, the shot spent so that it didn't cut or rip through her flesh, but made soft dents and pock marks.

Marshall would see his wife's ass and wonder if she knew what it looked like. If she did, why would she want to flash it at him, slipping the nighty off as she walked out of the den? Marshall was sitting in his leather chair trying to watch the eleven o'clock news. Tyra was showing him the lingerie she'd bought for the Mackinac Island convention weekend coming up. She'd leave the den, go out into the breakfast room or kitchen or somewhere, come back with another filmy outfit on — looking like a woman in a 1930s movie — and stand between Marshall and the television set with a hand on her hip and one fat leg in front of the other.

It was his own fault — before the news came on — expressing interest in Tyra's day. What'd you do? I went shopping. You didn't go out to the club? I'll show you what I bought. Did you talk to anybody? I'll be right back. Hey, while you're up, Marshall had said, do me a favor. Call

Mickey and find out when Frank's coming back. Tyra returned in a green chiffon baby-doll with green chiffon — bursting — bikini pants, asked Marshall if he liked it and got him to say he loved it before telling him no one answered at Dawson's.

"All right, this is the peach," Tyra said. "Which do you like better, the peach or the green?" The 165 pound model took a step and threw her hips, swirling the sheer material and giving Marshall a glimpse of the television screen.

"Which one do you like?"

"That one."

"Really? I thought you liked the green."

Crime. Governor Milliken urges suburbs to rescue the cities . . . whatever that meant. Marshall drew hard on his cigar, waiting.

"Do you love it or you just like it?"

"I love it," Marshall said.

"Why do you have it on so loud?"

"Leave it alone!"

"Ohhh, is her scairt?" Tyra petted her schnauzer who had perked up her little ears. Ingrid was lying in a deep leather chair, the twin to Marshall's.

Two pose as police in freeway holdup . . . commercials, the news again and Tyra was back.

"This is the Luci-Ann. You like it?"

"Fine."

"Don't ask what it cost, please." Tyra whirled and posed and fluffed the white marabou trimming that hung to the floor. "I'll tell you if you promise you won't be mad. Two hundred and seventy-five. But it's a Luci-Ann."

Three held in stabbing of woman on Belle Isle.

"Do you love it? . . . Marsh-*ull!* . . . Ohhh, I'm sorry, baby. I scairt her, din I? Does her like mommy's Luci-Ann?"

The schnauzer probably didn't give a shit one way or the other, but recognized a tone that could mean a doggie treat, sat up in the chair, pointed her little ears and yipped once.

A woman stabbed on Belle Isle and the suburbs asked to rescue the cities, in the recap. But no word about a woman in the suburbs missing, assaulted . . . or anything.

Marshall drew on the cigar until he could feel it in his jaw. The cigar was out. Frank and Bo were both out of town. Mickey . . . well, all he really knew, she wasn't home. Say she went to Beaumont. They fixed her up. Then, on the way home she stopped by a friend's. Or a friend took her to the hospital; that was it. Who was a close friend of Mickey's? He couldn't think of anyone immediately. Maybe Kay Lyons. He'd seen them sitting together talking. Charlie Lyons had said he'd be in Grand Rapids this week —

Tyra was out changing again.

Marshall raised his head. "Honey . . . call the Lyons for me, will you? Find out if Charlie's in town or when he's coming back. Will you do that, sweetheart?"

13

Melanie wore a long striped Arab dress, a headband and one of Frank's $30 ties for a belt. She seldom wore underwear or shoes. She was right there ready — practically at all times — lying on the sofa reading about people with style in *W*, a list of those who had it.

"Diana Vreeland."

"Never heard of her."

"Betty Bacall."

"You mean Lauren Bacall?" Frank said.

"Same one," Melanie said. "Yves St. Laurent."

"He's the guy that makes clothes, women's clothes."

"Georgia O'Keefe."

"Sounds like a stripper."

"Wrong. Giancarlo Giannini."

"Opera singer."

"Wrong. Jeanne Moreau."

"He's a . . . writer."

"She's an actress. Jerome Robbins."

"Who knows?"

"I'm giving you just the easy ones. Okay, Pat Buckley."

"He's the one, he was gonna punch that fag, what's his name, on TV."

"Pat's his wife . . . I think. Loulou de la Falaise."

"For Christ sake," Frank said.

They were in Frank Dawson's apartment, back from the casino. Melanie had won four-hundred-and-something playing roulette. Frank had dropped $3,200 at craps, not even shooting, betting against the shooter. He'd forgotten to call home and decided the hell with it, it was too late now, bedtime. Frank had his white loafers off, his shirt unbuttoned, relaxing, having one final Scotch. Melanie let her Coke sit on the coffee table. She lay curled up in a corner of the sectional sofa, holding *W* against her raised knees and taking his picture. He could see the underside of her long young thighs all the way to her exposed can. Or he could turn his head and look through the open sliding doors to the balcony and see imported palm trees in moonlight. They had brought them over from Florida to line the fairways, coconut palms that were slowly being overgrown with local scrub pine. The grounds-keepers would take a couple of hacks at the growth with machetes and stand around smoking cigarettes. It was getting harder to hire good people. The government in Nassau was crazy. He had to get out of here pretty soon. Move the account to Switzerland before the government took over everything and turned Fairway Manor into a post office or something.

"Jack Nicholson you know. Alain Resnais."

"Never heard of him."

"Here's one. Nicky Lauda."

"I don't know."

"He's a race-car driver. Jean Renoir."

"I don't want to play anymore."

There were things he didn't like about Melanie. She ought to comb her hair. She ought to clean up her language when they were out — sitting in the King's Inn cocktail lounge and seeing everybody turn around and look when she said, "Those fuckers, what do they know?" Things like that. She ought to bring her own toothbrush when she came here and quit using all his tranquilizers.

"One more. Yasmin Khan."

Still, Frank believed Melanie was one in a million. Maybe she was. At any given time there could be ten thousand or more healthy young Melanies lying on the beaches of the world, sitting at chic sidewalk tables with their backpacks stowed away, and each would be one in a million; though Frank would never realize there were so many. Melanie was from Santa Barbara, a California girl. She had been all over the Mediterranean, from Marbella to the Middle East. She had lived with a Hollywood director Frank had never heard of while the director was shooting a western in Spain. She had bunked with Italian film people at a Cannes Festival, moved onto Rome and Cinecittà with a second-assistant cameraman — bad for the image, moving down in the ranks — escaped to Piraeus and did the Greek islands on the motor-sailer of a dark little man who imported John Deere tractors, skipped down to Eilat — Israel's Miami Beach on the Gulf of Aqaba — with another film crew, no one in particular. Then, from Eilat to Copenhagen to London to Barbados to Freeport, Grand Bahama, where she'd finally had enough of her British photo-journalist friend, his quaaludes and rum, his cold sweats and crazy-talk in the middle of the night, and connected with Frank at Tano Beach over a bowl of conch chowder and a pint of dark, ten months ago. Mr. Frank A. Dawson from Detroit, with a bank account and development interests in the Bahamas. Melanie could read Frank's mind, anticipate his moods and keep him turned on without shifting into third gear. After some of the others, Frank was like a rest stop.

"George Balanchine."

"I'm gonna take that goddamn paper, whatever it is, and burn it."

"Meany. What do you want to do, fuck?"

"Well, since we're going to bed —" He couldn't get over the way she talked, but tried to react casually.

"You want to do the Florentine thing again?"

"What one was that?"

"You know, where we sit facing each other, my legs are over yours —"

"Yeah, that's a good one," Frank said. She was so offhand about it. Then in bed she'd talk real dirty, telling him what to do to her. Mickey never said a word. She'd lie there, get a little movement going, but not much. He'd roll over and she'd go in the bathroom for awhile, come back and ask him what he wanted for breakfast in the morning.

He said to Melanie, "I've filed."

She lowered the newspaper with her knees. "You have? Why didn't you tell me?"

"I talked to my lawyer Friday. He said it'll go out, she'll be served with the papers probably by Tuesday. Tomorrow."

"That's why you came early."

"Give her some time alone to think about it."

"What's she gonna do?"

"What do you mean, what's she gonna do? It's no-fault. She doesn't have anything to say about it."

"I mean how's she gonna take it?" Melanie said.

"I don't know. I don't really care." Frank got up. He went into the kitchen and came back with a fresh drink.

Melanie was waiting. "Will she be surprised?"

"I guess so."

"Will she cry . . . ask you not to do it?"

"I don't know. I don't think so. I think she'll go along with it. Oh, she'll say things to her friends, suck around for a little sympathy. Poor little thing — that prick, how could he? After she's been so good to him."

Melanie sat up, drawing her knees to her and wrapping her arms around them. "What's she like?"

"She's —" Frank had to think. He sipped his Scotch. "She's — what can I say? She's just kinda *there.* Nice looking, good figure. Everybody tells her how cute she is, you know, how does she stay so slim, all that."

"She good in bed?"

"Well, it's not really a big thing to her."

"No pun intended, huh?" Melanie said.

"It's not important to her. The way she was brought up, like a lot of the women we know, sex is something . . . they look at it as something you have to do when you're married. Something you have to put up with."

"That's weird," Melanie said.

"Well, you weren't brought up like that. How old were you, the first time you got laid?"

"Fourteen, I think. Yeah, fourteen. But I was giving hand jobs before that."

"My wife, these women we know, they lead a very sheltered life," Frank said. "The big thing they talk about at the club — well, some of them, they play golf, they're pretty active. But the others, along with my wife, the big thing to talk about would be what they're gonna cook for dinner."

"That's really weird," Melanie said. "I'd eat out."

"You don't eat out every night," Frank said. "No, you sit at the table, try and make conversation. I tell her about the business. It could be a problem I'm having with a sub-contractor, like trying to get the cement guy to come in when I need him —"

"Yeah?" Melanie said.

"She listens, but she doesn't give a shit. I try

and keep it light, tell her about my round of golf maybe if I played that day. No response."

"No response," Melanie said. "What's she interested in? You mind my asking?"

"No, I don't mind. What's she interested in?" Frank thought again. "How much I drink. She says, we go to a party and I'm a little high, she says your problem, you don't count your drinks. I say I did too count 'em. I had twenty-eight, exactly."

Melanie nodded and laughed.

"She doesn't think it's funny. I tell a joke, you know, like the one the guy gets bit on the pecker by the rattlesnake?"

Melanie grinned. "Yeah?"

"She doesn't think it's funny. Oh, she laughs. If other people are there she laughs, but she doesn't think it's funny. She's more interested in is the house clean? Or, where's Bo? It's late and Bo's not home yet. I say to her it's only ten-thirty, for Christ sake, he'll be home."

"What about your son? What's gonna happen?"

"That's something we'll have to discuss along with the settlement," Frank said. "She'll probably keep Bo, the mother, you know, I'm not gonna argue with that. It's all right, he and I'll see each other."

"I'd like to meet him," Melanie said.

"You probably will, you don't pack that big canvas bag and take off somewhere."

"Leave my place? I'm getting to be a homebody," Melanie said. "I've planted flowers — Hey, there was a guy renting the next apartment. He was there a couple of weeks with his wife. I was outside for a while, I went in, I just got in and he knocks on my door. I answer and he goes, 'I'll give you $500 if you'll take your clothes off and let me look at your body.' No shit."

"Just look? Come on —"

"No shit. I go, 'Hey, get fucked, okay?' Creepy guy —"

Yeah, Frank thought. She'd have the Arab dress off, or the string bikini, before the door closed. That was the only thing that bothered him. He had more than enough money to keep her happy, but she'd still fool around. He noticed the way she looked at young guys with flat stomachs and nice builds. They could be Bahamian, it didn't matter. If it ever bothered him too much or he ever caught her with somebody he'd end it, throw her out. He'd have to. It was her age. Pretty soon though, when she got to be twenty-two, twenty-three, she'd begin looking ahead and settle down. Growing flowers, that was a good sign.

They were in bed when the telephone rang, in semidarkness: lamplight from the living room on the floor; moonlight on the bed, the imported palm trees stirring outside the window. Frank raised his eyes, past the mound of her belly, past round pale breasts (her tummy-tum and her ninnies, he called them), to her face on the pillow. He raised his head then and her eyes opened.

She said, "Are we gonna answer it?"

"I don't know." Frank held his position, his can rounding over the foot of the bed, toes dug into the shag carpeting, a freestyler ready to dive. The phone continued to ring.

"You want me to?" Melanie said.

"No . . . I guess I better."

It could be Bo, something about the tennis camp he didn't like. It could be Mickey — because he'd forgotten to call earlier. Something about the car, playing helpless. Where should she get it fixed? Frank walked into the living room naked, scratching his crotch, feeling a little heft but nothing like he'd had before. That was all right, Melanie could get it back with one touch. She liked to touch it and talk to it, get down there and say dirty things to it softly. It was coming back already . . .

Then began to shrivel fast as the voice on the phone said, "How you doing, man? With that fine young lady you got with you —"

"Who is this?"

"Hold the line. Your wife wants to speak with you."

14

They had Mickey downstairs sitting in the straight chair by the telephone table with her mask on. Louis watched her fooling with her fingernails as she waited, as Ordell spoke into the phone. Louis and Ordell had their masks on, Louis holding a sheet of paper in his hand. Richard was wearing his monster face. Mickey was the only one in the room seated.

Ordell said, "I'm telling you the truth, man. Here she is." He looked over at Louis.

Louis watched him go to one knee and place the phone against Mickey's face. When her hands raised, he pushed them down. He'd hold it for her, his face close to hers. He touched her shoulder then, meaning for her to go ahead.

Mickey said, "Frank?"

Louis could hear the man's voice, some of the words, asking who that was and where was she and if this was her idea of a joke or what.

She said, "I don't know . . . Frank, listen to me . . . I don't *know!* They want you to hear my voice. That's all . . . No, I'm all right . . .

Frank, I don't *know* —"

Ordell put the phone against his chest. Richard took Mickey by the arm and led her across the room to the hallway and the stairs. Ordell looked at Louis and nodded to the chair. Louis shook his head. He took the phone from him, held it out as he looked at the sheet of paper in his other hand, then put the phone to his ear.

"Mr. Dawson," Louis said, "How you doing? And how's Melanie? I understand she's got great big ones." He looked over at Ordell and had to grin. Ordell was jiving his shoulders around with his elbows tucked in, not able to stand still. Louis put the phone against his chest and said, "He wants to know who this is."

Ordell had to turn away, laughing the way you did smoking grass when something that wasn't that funny forced the laugh out of you.

Louis said into the phone, "I'm not allowed to tell you, Mr. Dawson. But I can tell you this. Tomorrow go to the Providence Bank and Trust and draw a million dollars out of your account . . . Mr. Dawson? I think you better quit talking and listen, cause you're in deep shit, man. I want you to draw one million dollars in a cashier's check and deposit it at the same bank . . . you listening? To account number eight nine five double-oh thirty-nine." Louis waited. Ordell could hear the man's voice saying, "Hello? Hello?" Louis said into the phone, "You write it down? . . . Then get one." He waited again and repeated the number. "Now then, if the money's not deposited by noon tomorrow, you'll never see your wife again. If you go to the police . . . listen to me. You'll never see her again. You do anything but put the money in that account, your wife's gone, man. Gone." Louis hung up.

He said to Ordell, "How'd it sound?"

"No shit," Ordell said, "I was him, I be waiting for the bank to open."

"The only thing," Louis said, "what's he tell this Melanie? How tight you think he is with her?"

"She's ass, what she is," Ordell said. "He got her along for ass."

"I hope that's all," Louis said.

Louis sat in the dark with Mickey, without masks. He said, "Tomorrow afternoon'll be all over. You'll be home. It's not so bad, huh?"

She didn't answer him.

"Your son, he didn't go with him, did he?"

"He's in Florida, with my mother and dad."

"You know your husband had a girl with him down there?"

"No."

"You never suspected it?"

"No."

"You get along? You and your husband?"

"Why?"

"I'm just asking. Most men they go away, they pick up something. It isn't anything unusual."

"How did you know about her?"

"I can't tell you that," Louis said. "Your husband, he never mentioned her, uh? Like as a friend, or somebody that worked for him?"

"What's her name?"

"Melanie."

"That's cute," Mickey said. "No, I've never heard of her."

"You know about his bank account in Freeport?"

"He does business there. I assume he'd have an account."

"With over a million in it?"

"How do you know that?" Mickey said.

"We know," Louis said. "He knows we know. But you didn't, huh?"

"I don't know everything about his business. It's some kind of an investment corporation."

"Not this one," Louis said. "It's a private account. He's the only one in it."

"Maybe your information's wrong."

"It's the fifty grand a month he's been taking out of the apartments in Detroit," Louis said. "He's been going down there what, about two years?"

Mickey didn't answer. It was two and a half years, at least. Frank going to Freeport every month for a day or two while the Fairway Manor project was under way. Then, more recently, going for several days each month, working on land development with foreign investors, Frank had told her. This time the Japanese. He could have told her anything. But he hadn't said a word about apartment buildings in Detroit. She wondered if the man sitting in the rocker thought she was dumb.

The poor dumb wife who didn't know anything. God, still worried about keeping up appearances. What difference did it make what he thought?

She said, "Tell me about the apartments in Detroit," and listened to the man sitting in the rocker, hearing his words . . . her husband renovating apartment buildings with stolen materials and appliances . . . grossing at least a $100,000 a month, renting to pimps and prostitutes . . . taking out about half without reporting it as income, putting it away in a numbered bank account . . .

And the girl, Melanie (wondering what she looked like) . . .

Listening and realizing she had lived with a man fifteen years without knowing him. For the time being, Mickey was in her stunned period.

At seven-thirty Tuesday morning, Frank had a gin and grapefruit juice. Melanie made it for him — a weak one, he told her — and brought it to him on the balcony where he sat in a terry-cloth robe, a convalescent, staring at the deserted 18th fairway. He'd slept about an hour. He needed the drink in order to come down, relax, get his thinking in order. Melanie told him yes, it would be good for him. She knew enough to keep quiet but to be there, in a bleached-cotton caftan, watching him and willing to sympathize, encourage, as he began to rationalize.

He had told her about it because he had to tell someone, feel some kind of support, hear his thinking affirmed. He told himself she was intelligent, understanding — Then told her — this was incredible — his wife had been kidnapped, honest to God, and was being held for ransom. Melanie said, For how much?

She brought him another drink and said, Do you have any idea who they are? He said no. Could they be Bahamian? No. Could they have called from the island? No, he could tell by the connection it was long distance. Melanie waited a bit. She said, You can't risk going to the police, can you? He said no. She said, Even if you pay them, there's no assurance they would release her, is there? He said no. She said, You can't deal reasonably with people like that, take their word. You don't know what they might do. Weirdos, they could panic, they could be spaced out of their minds on something. She said, Frank, your wife might even be dead already. Do you realize that? He said it was possible. She said, You didn't tell me how much they want. He said, A million dollars. She said, to herself, Un-fucking-real, went inside to the bar and made him another drink and one for herself. For ten months she had been selling Frank short.

She kissed him on the cheek and sat down with him. The first of the early morning golfers were going by now, teeing off on 18.

Frank watched them. He said, "Keep your elbow in."

Melanie said, "You're cute, you know it?"

Frank said, "See, he hooked it."

She said wasn't it strange, filing for divorce and

then this happening? Not wanting to be married to her but, gosh, not wanting anything awful to happen to her either. At least if you could help it. The trouble was, they could do anything they wanted, couldn't they? They were in control. He supposed so. She said, You could pay them the million and they still might — rephrase that — you still might never see her again.

"Or what if I couldn't get to the bank for some reason?" Frank said. "I didn't make the payment in time?"

"Right. What would happen?"

"We don't know," Frank said. "We don't know if they mean it, do we?"

"We sure don't," Melanie said. She liked the sound of that "we" and said, "Well, we could call their bluff, see what happens."

"Can we risk it?" Frank said, thoughtful, staring down the fairway at the golf carts moving off.

"Turn it around," Melanie said. "I mean put yourself in their place. Where would you be if she was dead?"

Tuesday evening they let Mickey take a shower — she had to put on the same white slacks and blue cotton shirt — and gave her pot roast and noodles for supper. The one who had talked to her before, with the dark curly hair, came in to take the tray.

"If you're finished —" His voice was somewhat familiar — his quiet tone, his manner — but she couldn't be sure.

"Do you have today's paper? I wouldn't mind something to read."

"You aren't in it," Louis said. "You weren't on TV again either. I think your friend forgot about you."

Mickey said, "I thought I was going home this afternoon."

Louis didn't say anything right away. He put the tray down and came around to where she was sitting in the rocker and sat on the side of the bed, their positions reversed. He could see part of her face very faintly. She had seen his then, after the business with the masks. He didn't care. It was strange, downstairs with Ordell — even today, waiting all day, nothing — he felt pretty good. Upstairs, he felt depressed.

Louis said, "He hasn't paid yet."

"How is he supposed to do it? It might take time."

"No, that's not a problem."

"Can I ask how much you want?"

"A million," Louis said.

"A million *dollars?*"

"He's got it. I thought I told you that." There was a silence. Louis said, "What're you thinking? What happens if he doesn't pay?"

"What did you tell him you'd do?" Mickey said.

Louis hesitated. "We told him he'd never see you again." He stared at her face in the darkness. She didn't move, didn't make a sound. She seemed to be staring at him. He said, "Let me ask you. Is there any reason he won't?"

"I'm his wife," Mickey said.

"That's not an answer." Louis waited, but it was all the answer he got.

Ordell was on the phone. Louis went into the kitchen and dropped the tray in the sink and told Richard to get some putty and fix the goddamn holes in the doors. How many times was he supposed to tell him? Richard said, "I'm eating." He sure was, sitting with his bare arms on the kitchen table, head low to the plate, shoveling with a biscuit and sucking in the noodles. Ordell appeared in the doorway and Louis went out to the living room with him.

"Mr. Walker say the man's up in his apartment, hasn't left the place all day. The young lady went out, bought two bags of groceries at Winn-Dixie, like they gonna hole up there."

"Maybe he phoned the bank."

"*I* phoned the bank," Ordell said. "Wasn't any deposit made."

"I mean since then," Louis said.

"Bank closed at three o'clock."

"Maybe he's sick," Louis said. "It could've affected him, his nerves maybe."

"It's gonna affect his wife what it's gonna affect," Ordell said.

"Well, call him again," Louis said. "What can you do?"

"Have her say something?"

"Yeah, let him hear her voice again. See if we can get the guy off his ass." Louis said then, "That goddamn Nazi, he still hasn't fixed the holes."

"Here, look," Frank said. He clicked his silver pencil and jotted figures on the back of a magazine, in a clear section of a Marlboro ad, as he continued. "The building costs a hundred grand. I put about forty-grand worth of materials and appliances in it and have it reappraised at *two*-hundred grand."

"Wow," Melanie said, crouched next to his chair, his little girl, resting her chin on his arm.

"Okay. I've only put ten per cent down, right? And the forty-grand worth of materials only cost me about four or five grand. But I'm writing off depreciation on *two*-hundred grand. Then, on the rentals, I only declare about sixty-per cent occupancy. It's all paid in cash —"

The phone rang and he stopped.

"Excuse me," Melanie said. She went over to the marble-top dry bar that was open, the louvered doors pushed back to show bottles and crystal, and picked up the phone.

"Mr. Dawson's residence." She waited a moment. "I'm sorry, but Mr. Dawson's out. Would you care to leave a message? . . . No, I'm afraid you're mistaken. Mr. Dawson left the island earlier today and didn't say when he'd return. Good night —" in a pleasant telephone voice. She hung up.

"I used to be a receptionist for a p.r. guy in Los Angeles. He was a real asshole, a friend of my father's, but I met some interesting people."

"At the moment I'm a little more interested in

who just called," Frank said. He was feeling mellow and didn't sound drunk, though he showed it when he weaved from his favorite chair on his trips to the bathroom and, coming back, would make a dive at Melanie if she happened to be on the sectional sofa that could be arranged to form a playpen. The apartment was done in shades of beige and neutral raw silk, with touches of wicker and aluminum and graphics Melanie had picked up at the International Village.

"He really didn't say anything. He asked for you, then said he knew you were here."

"How would he know that?"

"He's guessing."

The phone rang again, several times before Melanie picked it up.

"Hello." She waited, listening, picking at the front of her white caftan. "That's very interesting, but I can't very well put him on, sport, if he isn't here, now can I?" She was losing her receptionist manner. "Yes, it is. And who are you?" She listened again, rolling her eyes now. "I'm sorry, he's gone and didn't say when he'd be back. Ciao." She hung up.

"He knew my name."

"What'd he say?"

"He said your wife wanted to talk to you. So —"

"She was on the phone?"

"No, it sounded like a black guy. He said tell him his wife wants a word with him."

Frank was thoughtful, silent now.

"So what does that tell us?" Melanie said. "They can be faked out. You didn't pay and they haven't done anything about it."

The phone rang again.

"I better talk to them," Frank said. He put his hands on the chair arms to push himself up.

Melanie raised the receiver and then replaced it, breaking the connection. She said, "What did we decide, Frank?"

"I know, but — maybe if I talked to them I could find out who they are."

"What difference does it make? If you start listening to them — it's like with hijackers and the PLO and all those guys. You start to give in, Frank, and they've got you. You don't have anything to say to them, do you?"

"I guess not," Frank said.

"I don't know, I had a feeling," Louis said. "But you're the one had it first. Somebody in it you hadn't planned on, you didn't know about. I guess that started me thinking."

"She pick up the phone, they no way to get past her."

"Well, he's sitting there," Louis said. "She isn't doing it by herself. So — what're they doing?"

"Seeing if we serious," Ordell said. "We got to impress it on the man some way. Go down there and sit on him, say look here . . . show him something, huh, like maybe his wife's baby finger."

"He knows we got her," Louis said.

"Im*press* it on him. Hey, we serious."

"Either he cares what happens to her or he doesn't give a shit," Louis said. "The finger isn't gonna do anything. He gives *us* the finger. Stick it." He didn't like to hear Ordell talking that way. Maim the woman for nothing, that wasn't a good idea. That was getting into something else and it would no longer be clean and simple. "But you're right," Louis said. "We got to put him against the wall."

"So we go down there," Ordell said. "Leave Richard with her."

Richard, Louis thought, Jesus. He said, "If you go, you got this guy Cedric Walker. I mean if you go alone and I stay here. I think one of us's got to be with her and not just Richard. In fact I'm gonna insist on it."

"You want to stay, that's cool," Ordell said. "I'll do it. Me and Mr. Walker." Ordell thought a moment, watching Louis. "You worried about Richard?"

"No, we get along. If I don't have to talk to him."

"Then you got nothing to worry about, have you?"

"No, I'm not worried about anything," Louis said. "I've never been happier in my life."

15

Melanie rose to her elbows brushing hair from her eyes, the tips of her bare breasts resting on the lounge, and said, “Hey!” to the black guy walking off with her straw bag. She was alone at the pool and saw, now, there were two of them.

“You mind?”

“I’m jes going in the shade here,” Ordell said. He took the straw bag with the big blue and pink straw flowers on it to the patio bar beneath the thatched roof and began feeling through it.

“You can have the money and the Coppertone and the Kleenex, but leave my wallet, okay? I just got the driver’s license. It took me months.”

Ordell came back with the straw bag in one hand and her keys in the other. He dropped the bag on the cement and sat down on the edge of the lounge, looking at her through his Spectra-Shades. “He upstairs? Or has he still left the island?”

“Oh,” Melanie said.

Ordell smiled a little. “Yeah, oh.”

“It’s the truth, he’s not here. I’m staying at his place while he’s gone.”

Ordell threw the keys underhand to the other man, a Bahamian. Melanie strained a little higher, turning her head to the side. She recognized the man's tight gray pants, very tight, with no hips, and the pink shirt, the man walking off through the shrubs toward the front of the building. Cedric, yes. She had met him at Churchill's or The Pub, one of those places.

"You getting red marks all over your titties from the chair," Ordell said.

"They rub off," Melanie said. "Listen, I know the other guy. If you want to chat, fine, but if I lose any teeth over this it's Cedric's ass, because sooner or later I'll call the cops."

Ordell frowned, hurt. "Lose some teeth?"

"So we understand one another," Melanie said. "Or if I'm not around at dinner time and my mother starts worrying. The island isn't that big you can hide somebody very long."

"I found that out," Ordell said. "I came down here about seven, eight years ago. I had some money to spend, I said hey, go down to a paradise island and have some of those big rum drinks and watch the natives do all that quaint shit beating on the oil drums, you know?"

Melanie watched him, one eye closed in the sun. She seemed interested.

"I got to the hotel out at West End," Ordell said. "I register, ask for my room key. The man say, We don't have no room keys. He say, No, you don't lock your room in the Bahamas, mon, we honest people. See, this was some time ago.

It's all changed now. I said to myself, Hey, shit. I look in some rooms during the time I was there. Sure enough, all the rooms, the people leave their stuff on the dresser, some in the open suitcases, some of them stick the wallets and travelers' checks under the socks, you know?"

Melanie nodded, one eye still closed. "You rip 'em off?"

"Noooo, I didn't rip nothing. I say to my man Cedric Walker the bone-fisherman I met, Hey, you understand all the bread they is, all the loot laying around here waiting on you? He say, What? I say, Money, honey, sitting on the dressers. He say, Oh. Say, You take all that stuff, mon, where you take it to? I say, You take it home, baby. Give some to mama."

Melanie said, "That's wild."

"But he say, No. You got money, you got a new watch, they see it, the police, everybody see it. What you going to do, bury it? So nobody see it? I said to him, Then go some place else —"

Ordell looked up. Melanie followed his gaze to see Cedric Walker coming back through the shrubs.

"Mr. Walker the bone-fisherman," Ordell said, "he take me all the way to the other side of the island where you see jes rocks there and sand and the waves coming in. Nothing. He say to me, Here. I say, Here what? He say, Here is some place else. Here is as far as some place else is . . . You understand what I'm saying?"

"That's wild," Melanie said. She saw Cedric

Walker shake his head. "Didn't believe me, did you?"

"Wasn't I didn't believe you," Ordell said. "I had to satisfy my mind. You understand? Now put your top on, we gonna go some place."

They drove over to Lucaya in Cedric Walker's '72 Vega, Ordell looking at the hotels and the gambling casino and the cars driving on the wrong side of the parkway, Melanie looking down at the way Cedric Walker's leg filled out his light-gray pants and the vein that popped in his forearm when he worked the gearshift.

At the marina, walking along the cement to Mr. Walker's 20-foot Boston Whaler, Melanie said, "There isn't any place around here you have to get to by boat."

"To get out in the ocean you do," Ordell said.

He and Melanie sat aft on green life-preserver cushions while Mr. Walker stood amidships at the wheel, his face raised to the spray, enjoying it, the square bow of the Whaler slapping through the waves as they headed out Bell Channel, passing the charter boats coming in for the day. Melanie didn't say anything until Ordell stood up and took her by the arms. She said, "What the fuck — hey, come on, *don't!*" as he threw her over the side.

Cedric maintained his heading for a hundred meters or so, then brought the whaler around in a wide arc, into the sundown sky beyond Pinder Point, cut the revs to a low rumble and let the boat drift toward the head of hair glistening in the water.

When the boat was close, Ordell, leaning on the gunwales, said, "You want to tell me where the man's at?"

In the car, driving back to Freeport, Melanie sat in the back seat with Ordell. He said he didn't mind, she could get him wet. She was a good girl. She was a nice *big* girl, all clean and shiny from her swim in the ocean. Yes, she could take them to this friend's house where Mr. Dawson was spending the day, sort of getting away from everything. Or, Ordell offered, they could go back to Mr. Dawson's place and call him, tell him to come home, huh? That sounded like the way to do it, instead of walking in somebody's house not knowing who was home. At Fairway, Mr. Walker waited in the car while Ordell and Melanie went up to the beige-and-white top-floor apartment with the playpen sofa.

Ordell looked around while Melanie put on her caftan and pulled the string bikini out from under it. "Like magic," Ordell said. "Go ahead, call him."

"I've got something to tell you first," Melanie said, "I think's gonna mess up your scam, but don't blame me, okay? It's the timing."

"What's the timing?" Ordell said.

"He filed for divorce two days before he came down."

Ordell waited. "Yeah?"

"And you tell him he'll never see his wife again?"

Ordell didn't move or say anything.

"He doesn't *want* to see her again," Melanie said. "You're doing him a favor. You're saving him about a hundred grand a year in alimony."

"He say that?"

"He doesn't have to, I know him. He's telling himself right now there's nothing he can do. If you kill his wife it won't be his fault. You told him not to go to the cops; that's one out, he can say he was worried about her safety, right? And legally, he can tell himself he's not supposed to deal with extortionists. So if he does nothing he's free and clear."

"The man come right out and *say* he want his wife dead?"

"He won't *say* anything. He wants it to happen without his thinking about it."

"Now wait a minute" — Ordell had to slow it down — "what if we let her go?"

Melanie shrugged. "He goes home and gets his divorce." She paused. "But where does that leave you? He won't involve the cops, for reasons you undoubtedly know. But she'll call them in a minute. Then where are you?"

"She hasn't seen us."

"Come on," Melanie said, "you don't know what she's seen, or what she might've heard. You've got guys working with you — maybe she identifies one of them, and if the cops've got any kind of sheet on you I'll bet you're picked up in two days."

Ordell kept staring at her. "You ever been busted?"

"Just dope a couple of times. Possession."

"But you know a few things, been there and back, huh? And what you're wondering most," Ordell said, "is what's gonna happen to *you.*"

Melanie smiled, giving him an easy shrug, and moved to the marble-top bar. "It passed through my mind. You want a drink?"

"Something with rum," Ordell said.

"Rum and coconut and pineapple," Melanie said and got busy, pouring ingredients and crushed ice into a blender. Ordell came over next to her, put a hand on her hip and let it slide over her nice young fanny.

"So where are we? Seeing how you're way ahead."

"Well, I presume you've looked into simple extortion," Melanie said. "He pays or you report him to the IRS."

"I don't see we could prove anything."

"No, but you could probably dump a shitload of trouble on him and some very bad publicity.

"What's that worth?"

"Well, first of all you're out of your skull asking for a million bucks. He may have it, but there's no way in the world you could get that much transferred without the Bahamian government getting involved. I mean somebody *in* the government, in finance. They'll tie you up so tight with authorizations and fees, you'd be lucky to get a few thousand off the island, if that."

"It's snowing out," Ordell said.

"Hey, you're not getting it anyway, you might as well quit dreaming and be realistic. So okay, it looks like a bummer. But maybe — and that's all I'm saying — *maybe* you can still get *some*thing out of it. I mean you're this far, it'd be a shame if you didn't."

Ordell rubbed her nice can gently. "Is this my new partner I'm talking to?"

"I'd just as soon keep it you do your thing and I do mine," Melanie said. She handed him a frothy drink in a brandy snifter the size of a bowl. "I don't know what my thing is yet. It may be long term, I may settle for a little scratch and move on, I don't know. But I'm willing to cooperate with you because I like you and because I don't want to end up in the fucking ocean. It's that simple."

"Cooperate how?" Ordell sipped his drink, leaving a trace of white froth on his mustache. Melanie wiped it off with the tip of her finger and licked it.

"I was thinking something like — how about if you disappeared for a hundred grand? I think I could talk something around that figure and get him to think it's his idea. For his peace of mind."

"Isn't a million, is it?" Ordell said.

"No, it isn't a sack of wet shit either," Melanie said.

"I got a partner, few others, have to pay them their wages."

"Well, how you handle that, it's up to you. You could pick up the money — you could be in Paris the same day, let your friends collect unemployment. That's up to you," Melanie said. "The only thing he would have to be sure of before, I mean

Mr. Dawson, he'd have to be sure he's never gonna see his wife again."

Ordell put the drink down on the marble top and passed the back of his hand over his mouth, taking his time.

"For the hundred grand," Ordell said, "you're not saying disappear. You're saying kill the man's wife."

"Unh-unh. I'm saying, when he learns his wife's dead, you get a hundred grand. Maybe even a hundred and a half. I'm not saying you have to do it," Melanie said. "Isn't there someone you could call?"

16

Thursday morning, the first couple of times Ordell phoned Richard's house, Louis answered and Ordell hung up hearing his voice. The third time he called, by then about twelve-thirty, Richard answered. This was the Freeport-Detroit conversation:

Ordell: Finally. Where's Louis?

Richard: I'll get him —

Ordell: No! Richard, wait! . . . Richard? Listen, I'll tell you and you can tell him. It's all set, man. It's done. You gonna be able to go to California, Richard.

Richard: Boy, that's good to hear. It's all set, huh?

Ordell: Yeah, taken care of. Home free, man.

Richard: Somebody called twice, and hung up. We don't know who it was.

Ordell: Don't worry about it, it's cool, Richard. Listen now what I want to tell you. Listen very carefully, Richard. It's the most important thing has to be done.

Richard: Just a minute, I'll be right back —

Ordell: RICHARD!

Richard: I got to turn the fire down under the cabbage.

(Ordell waited in the phone booth in the lobby of the King's Inn, ten dollars worth of quarters stacked on the metal shelf.

(The way Ordell saw it, Louis would be against the idea. In fact, Louis would kick and scream if he even knew about it. So why cut him in? Louis was a nice person, but it was a different whole new deal now. He had to tell Richard something to tell Louis. Then he had to get Richard to do the job and not fuck it up. All this over the phone in the hot phone booth. It wasn't going to be easy. But whoever said picking up a hundred and fifty grand was? That going to Paris, France, sounded pretty good, you know it? Send Louis a postcard . . .)

Richard: Hello?

Ordell: Your cabbage all right?

Richard: It was boiling over, but I got it.

Ordell: Louis upstairs, Richard?

Richard: He's always upstairs. I think he's screwing her, but when I go up there they aren't doing it.

Ordell: Richard, tonight . . . I want you to take the lady home.

Richard: I think he screws her real fast and doesn't take his pants off or anything.

Ordell: Richard! (pause) You have to listen to me, man, very very carefully. You listening?

Richard: Yeah, I'm listening.

Ordell: Since we all through, I want you and Louis to take the lady home tonight.

Richard: Tonight take her?

Ordell: Tonight when it's dark. Tell Louis to get a car like he did and put her in the trunk. You follow in your car, Richard, case he has a flat tire or something. You understand? See, my van's at the airport, Richard. But you don't want to use it anyway. Always, Louis say, steal a car. It's a rule.

Richard: He gets a car and I follow him in my Hornet.

Ordell: In the black Hornet. Tell Louis, take her in the house, lock her in a closet and cut the phone wires so he'll have time to get way away from there — you understand? — and she can't call anybody. But then, Richard?

Richard: What?

Ordell: This next part you got to do without Louis knowing about it. You got to when he's gone, Louis's gone, you go back to her house . . . go in . . . find out where he put her so you don't have to look all over for her, you understand?

Richard: Yeah, find out where he put her.

Ordell: Then, Richard . . . you have to kill her.

Richard: (pause) I do?

Ordell: You have to, Richard, on account of she knows who you are. She told me. She said she recognize your voice and saw your pants. She know you the one came to her house. That's what the Jew lady told me, Richard. She said you ain't getting away with this, cause I know who that fat son of a bitch rent-a-cop is and I'm gonna see him put in jail.

Richard: You know I wondered about that. There was something she said —

Ordell: We don't have no choice, Richard. I don't want to see you, any of us go to jail. Man, it'll kill you, worse than kill you in there with all those perverts, man, taking all kinds of trips on you. Richard . . . you got to kill the Jew lady. There ain't no other way.

Richard: Well — (long pause) What should I use?

Ordell: You the expert, Richard. (pause) But, Richard, listen to me. Don't . . . tell . . . Louis. He'll chicken on you, Richard, and mess you up.

Richard: I think the Python, the mag. It's my favorite. (pause) You know something?

Ordell: What, man?

Richard: I knew she was a Jew. I could tell.

17

Neatness counts. Of all the rules of magazine contests Mickey had entered when she was young, that was the one she remembered. She had taken it upon herself to be neat and clean long before she learned about virgins and holy purity from the I.H.M. Sisters. When she was a little girl, her mother had told her, she used to change clothes three and four times a day. She would come downstairs wearing a good dress to go out to play and her mother would march her back up to her room.

The blue shirt and white slacks didn't look that bad, for four days. She was pretty sure she didn't smell. They had let her take a shower yesterday and the day before. But there was no deodorant in the bathroom, obviously. The fat policeman didn't seem to know what it was. He hadn't forgotten to bring it, this was his house — he had said it to the nice one outside the bathroom door, arguing, "It's my house, ain't it?" — though she couldn't associate the fat policeman with this room. It was more like her grandmother's. And then her mother was mixed up in her mind with the fat policeman.

What would her mother think if she knew? Her father — she had never realized it before — her father looked like a TV dad in his cardigan sweater with the full sleeves, his pipe, his gray hair — thin but still wavy — his comfortable manner. Her dad would look at the fat policeman and say, "Hi, chief, how are you?" She would say, "Dad, he kidnapped me." And her mother would say, "Oh, now, you're imagining things. You can see he's a policeman." And her father would wait on the sidelines with his pipe while she and her mother discussed it. Both her mother and dad would accept the policeman, and his authority, at face value. She could not imagine them questioning anything — other than the Democratic Party and trade unions — or discussing or arguing with each other about anything . . . *important*.

What was important?

To get some clean clothes, go home, look at the house . . . call to see how Bo was — She stopped and thought: You're as bad as they are. Stay in your own little world —

She thought, If you get out of this, what will you do? What will you say to Frank?

Come on, you walk in the house and he's standing there. What will you say? . . . Hi? She heard a pretend little-Mickey voice say, "Oh, hi . . . No, I'm fine. How're you?" And never discuss it beyond that point ever again. Hide at the club and get back into the routine. "No, I haven't been away really. I was —" Where?

There were two quick raps on the door, the sound of the key in the lock. Mickey turned off the bed lamp and sat down in the rocker. The nice one came in from the hallway light with the dinner tray. She had heard the fat policeman this morning, but not the other one, the black one, since the day before yesterday.

"What time is it?"

"About one," Louis said. He placed the tray on the bed.

"I don't think I can eat any more noodles."

"Ham and cabbage today," Louis said.

"I'm not hungry."

"And cream-style corn."

"Oh, that's different," Mickey said, "cream-style corn. Do you people read? I'd love something to read."

"You're going home," Louis said.

Mickey sat up, her hands on the chair arms. "When?"

"Later on."

"He paid you?"

"We're gonna drop you off after awhile."

Mickey sat back in the chair again, slowly. "I don't believe you."

"So, don't," Louis said. He turned to go out.

"Wait — Did my husband really pay you?"

"Yeah, it's done."

"All you asked for?"

"I guess he must've."

"But you're not sure?"

"Yeah, I'm sure." He motioned to the tray. "Eat your dinner."

"What're you going to do to me? Will you tell me?"

"I already did. You're going home."

"I won't tell anybody," Mickey said. "I promise I won't go to the police."

"Well, it wouldn't help your husband any," Louis said. "I 'magine you'll have a few things to say to him but I'd keep in mind he's paid a lot of money for you."

"Did you talk to him?"

"Not personally, but it's all done. I 'magine you'll have a few things to say to your friend, too. I'd like to hear what he's telling people, how he got the cut in his head."

She was thinking, Could it actually be happening this way? Go home, pick up where she left off. It was what she had been thinking about just before. Walking in the house and seeing Frank, saying, Hi-I'm-fine-how're-you — ?

She said again, "I don't believe you. It doesn't happen like this."

"What doesn't?"

"It doesn't happen as if it *never* happened, for God sake. You can't kidnap somebody and take a million dollars and that's the end of it."

"It is if it works," Louis said.

"Do you have the money?"

Louis hesitated. "I told you, yes."

"You've seen it?"

"Look, take my word. You're going home."

Her voice rose. "No!" Then was quiet again, though with an edge to it. "Something's going on. It doesn't *happen* this way. And you don't know any more than I do. The other one went to Freeport, didn't he?"

"I got to go downstairs," Louis said.

"He called you and said my husband gave him the money? It was that simple?"

"I'll be back for you," Louis said.

"To kill me?"

He stopped, his hand on the door. "Take it easy, okay? I say you're going home, you're going home."

In the kitchen Louis said, "The one thing I don't understand, why he didn't ask to talk to me."

"He was in a phone booth," Richard said.

Louis waited, but that was all the explanation he was going to get. "What did he say exactly?"

"I told you."

"I mean his exact words. Like if you were writing a police report."

"He said, it's all set."

"All set, uh?" What did "all set" mean. It could mean anything. "You should've called me to the phone."

Richard tightened up. "He said *I* could tell you it was all set and take the woman home, and then about getting a car and putting her in the trunk, that part, that was all he said. He didn't say anything else, goddarn-it!"

"What're you getting mad about?"

"I ain't mad," Richard said. "I say something, it's the truth." With his face red, his mouth a tight line, looking as though he was going to punch somebody out.

Big dumb fuckhead Nazi gunfighter to handle, to keep calm, keep him busy making his fucking noodles. Louis said, trying to sound like Ordell, "Hey, it's cool, Richard. Nothing to be upset about, man. I believe you. I just want to make sure I understand it. You know what I mean?"

"He said it was all set, he had the money."

"Ah," Louis said. "I must've missed that part. He did get the money. Good. See, I was wondering about that." You dumb fuckhead. "So, what I want to do now, I want to use your car for a little while. Line up some transportation for tonight."

"How long you want to use it?"

"Half hour maybe. That okay?"

Richard guessed it was, but took his time giving Louis his keys. Then told Louis when he came back, he was to *back* the Hornet in the driveway like he found it. Richard liked it headed out at the street, ready.

Louis almost told him to stay away from the lady: they didn't want to get her mad and upset now that it was over. But he thought better of it and kept his mouth shut. He'd hurry instead.

In fact, Louis decided, once he was out on Woodward Avenue in the Hornet, he might be able to get back in about five minutes.

His original plan was to go north into Ferndale

and Royal Oak; but then he got the restaurant idea and couldn't think of a good one north, with valet service, within ten miles. There was a good one about a mile and a half south though, the Paradiso. He could walk there from Richard's house, later on when it was dark. Go in the parking lot, spot a car in the back row, describe it to the parking guy and hand him a buck. It was a lot easier than crossing wires. And he wouldn't have to go scouting around and leave Richard alone with the lady.

What he'd do, check the distance to the restaurant on the odometer to make sure it wasn't farther than he thought or had burned down or anything. If it was still there, he should be back in about five minutes easy.

Try it again. You walk in the house — Mickey pictured it, opening the door, seeing the familiar black-and-white tile. You go into the kitchen. There's a sound from the den. Frank comes out. He sees you, stops. His hands come up. He says . . .

Quietly — no, gravely, his hands at his sides. "How are you?" And you say, "I'm fine, thank you." Very coolly, looking him right in the eye. "And how was Freeport?" And Frank says . . . "Not bad. I shot a seventy-two at Lucaya yesterday. The greens were slow, otherwise —"

"Do you want something to eat? I haven't been to the store this week, but we must have something." She goes to the refrigerator.

Her mother was there, somewhere, saying, "Oh, Margaret, don't be silly. Frank wouldn't do that. Frank's a wonderful husband and father." While her dad, holding his pipe, watched. "No, mom, really. Things are not as nice as they seem. Nothing is." But why bother? It would require too much of an effort to tell her mother, to tell her friends at the club. And for what? Assuming they would let her go. She would sit and wait and see and if they did she couldn't tell anyway. Frank would go to jail.

Try that.

"Keep your mouth shut, Frank. You say one more word about your golf game, I'll turn you in."

It was getting better.

Richard entered his mother's room without the monster mask on, without knocking and telling the woman to turn out the light first. He walked in, looked at her sitting in the rocker and then at the tray of food on the bed. Sure as hell just what he thought, she hadn't touched it.

He said, "You didn't eat your ham."

"I'm not hungry."

"I forgot you're not allowed to eat it."

He lifted the tray and took it over to the dresser, Mickey giving him a funny look "Why aren't I allowed to eat it?"

"Your religion, if you want to call it that. I call it something else."

She wondered if it was worth asking him what

he was talking about . . . and why he'd left the light on and wasn't wearing the rubber Frankenstein face she had seen once through the uncovered eye of her mask. She watched him come around to the near side of the bed — in his policeman pants and a white T-shirt, hands on his hips, the armpits stained gray — and tried not to breathe.

"He tell you, Louis, you're going home?"

Louis. "Yes, he did." The nice one was Louis.

"I'm gonna miss you around here."

"I'll miss you too," Mickey said. "I've had a lovely time." The wrong thing to say, making fun of him. Seeing his nose tighten, seeing Richard's hard-eyed look-right-through-'em look.

He pulled her up by the arms and threw her on the bed, moving in over her as she tried to twist free, as she strained, turning her head from the red face looking down at her, feeling his knee between her legs. He was telling her now he had been wanting to see something and he was gonna see it, goddarn-it, and he was gonna do whatever he wanted and she was gonna lie there and not move or holler or anything or he would kill her right now, right here on his mother's bed, and not wait till after. Her eyes were closed. She was trying to get her breath and trying to remember what she was supposed to do that it said in books and on the women's page. Fight him. Kick him in the balls. Or was it don't fight him? Let it happen. She could not imagine letting it happen. She could not imagine that it would be possible for it to happen. He would tear her, injure her —

He rose, pulling her to a sitting position on the side of the bed. “Take your clothes off or I’ll rip ’em off you,” Richard said, and began unfastening the heavy, gold-plated Wells Fargo buckle on his belt.

Mickey looked down unbuttoning her shirt, chin to chest, seeing the whiteness of her bra, still snowy white, and the tiny pink bow between the cups. Little Mickey sitting there. The real Mickey perched above watching, thinking, The pink bow is too much. Thinking, The poor girl. Seeing Frank come in naked from the bathroom with a towel over his arm. Seeing 6-4 Marshall Taylor stoop-shouldered naked, vaguely, Marshall there and gone. Thinking, What would Susan Brownmiller do? Thinking, Get it over with. She took her shirt off.

“Now the bra-zeer,” Richard said.

Her hands went behind her, unhooked the bra and pulled if off. My God, her nipples were sticking out.

“Now your pants and your undies,” Richard said.

He was standing with his uniform trousers around his ankles, showing his round, marble-white thighs, thumbs hooked in his Jockeys, ready to push them down. The Mickey up above said, You poor little thing. I’d take my chances and kick him in the balls.

And was totally surprised when nice Mickey on the bed rolled back, came forward with momentum, eyes on Richard’s crotch, and with a grunt and all the force she had drove her foot into the sagging pouch of his Jockeys.

Unbelievable, Richard saying, "Unnnngh!" doubling over, holding his groin, little Mickey rolling off the bed, grabbing her shirt, doing it almost as a reflex action — the shirt and the bra with it — running through the door and down the stairs, almost down the stairs —

Louis — she remembered his name — was near the bottom, already on the steps looking up at her.

Louis said, "Jesus Christ." Louis knew. One look at her, bare-chested, holding the shirt, Richard nowhere downstairs. He said, "Come on. Come *on!*" Reached up and tried to grab her arm as she held the shirt tightly against her. "Where is he?"

"In the room."

They heard Richard then, from upstairs, screaming, "Come back'n this room! You hear me!"

"Jesus Christ," Louis said. "Come on."

She was into her shirt, holding it closed, ran out the front door and down to the walk, hearing Louis yell at her to get in the car, and turned and ran toward the driveway, cutting after him through the low hedge. The car was pointed toward the street. Inside, Louis fumbled with the keys. He got the right one into the ignition and started the car and she heard the fat one's voice again. "Get back in here!"

The car was moving. It shot down the driveway and Mickey held onto the seat and the door handle because the turn into the street would be abrupt, wrenching. But the car didn't turn, it kept going — Louis pressing down on the accelerator — straight for the chainlink fence across the street, into a driveway toward closed double gates in the fence and a yellow sign that said FAIRGROUNDS PARKING USE GATE NO. 5.

The blue-and-white Detroit Police cruiser rolled past Grayling Elementary School on Bauman — a woman's voice crackling on the radio — reached the corner and came to a stop. After a pause the cruiser turned left onto State Fair.

The Detroit patrolman, looking straight ahead through his windshield, saw the black car come out of the drive halfway up the block and knew he was about to hear tires scream through a turn and if the guy didn't sideswipe some cars and pile up he'd be on him before he hit Woodward, nail him with the gumballs flashing blue and siren turned up to high yelp. Christ Almighty, but the car kept going. Smashed through the horse-trailer gate, smashed right through it, the cyclone swing-gates flying apart and the black car heading north through the empty fairgrounds. It looked good, it looked to be something different for a change.

The Detroit patrolman flipped on his Super Fireballs, took the radio mike off the hook.

Before he could say a word he heard the gunfire . . . saw the fat guy on the porch, the guy holding his belly and blazing away with a revolver, shooting at the black car running away, the car nearly gone. Where in the hell was it? Up by the animal barns already.

The Detroit patrolman said to his mike, eyes staring through the windshield, "Seven four four two . . . in the 1,000 block of State Fair east of Woodward. Request immediate backup. We got some kind of wild asshole here firing a revolver."

There were traces of yellow paint on the grille of the Hornet, from the sign that told about parking at Gate No. 5, the gate the car came darting out to turn right into Woodward Avenue. Seconds later they were cresting the overpass at Eight Mile Road, moving north into the suburbs. The Salem cigarette billboard against the sky, higher than the overpass, told them it was exactly 1:55.

Mickey had buttoned her shirt. She held her bra balled in both hands, her hands resting in her lap. She said, "Where're you taking me?"

"Where'm I taking you?" Louis looked at her, surprised. "I'm taking you home."

Neither of them spoke or looked at each other after that. They seemed interested in the traffic and the franchised food places, the drive-ins and car-dealer lots, moving through Ferndale, Royal Oak, Pleasant Ridge, some more of Royal Oak, out past the Mile Roads toward Birmingham and Bloomfield Hills.

In a little while Louis began to relax. He felt relieved. He didn't want to think about anything right now. He saw familiar signs and places, N & S Automotive. He began thinking of Mopars and Chevies and a '64 Barracuda with a blown Hemi in the rear end, "Hemi Under Glass," one of the first of the dragstrip showcars that did wheelies. He had seen it out at Detroit Dragway . . . on the way to Toledo . . . you went past on I-75 all the way to Miami. Then came back.

He said, "Right here, this stretch of North Woodward, used to be called the street-racing capital of the world. You know that?"

Mickey looked at him then. She said, "I don't want to go home."

18

Louis tried to imagine explaining it to Ordell.

"What was I supposed to do, tell her get out of the car?"

Ordell would say, "*Yes.* She wouldn't get out, you *push* her out."

He'd say, "I know but, she didn't have any shoes on. She was sitting there holding her bra all bunched up. I didn't know where else to take her. She looked like she was in a daze and I couldn't think of any place."

Ordell would say to their lawyer, "This man's crazy. He's gonna get out for being mentally retarded and I'm gonna get ten to twenty-five."

Louis took Mickey to Ordell's big four-bedroom apartment overlooking Palmer Park. He sat her down in the living room in the La-Z-Boy, put her bare feet up on the Magic Ottoman that rose out of the chair and got her a vodka and tonic. She drank it down in about two minutes and he got her another one. She didn't ask where they were; she didn't ask him anything. She still seemed in a daze. Louis got himself a drink and put his feet on the coffee table where the box of Halloween masks was still sitting, now with a bunched-up bra lying next to the box. They sat there for awhile and didn't say anything.

What happened after that, during the afternoon and evening, Ordell wouldn't believe it if he told him.

Mickey started talking.

She said, "I don't know what to do. I don't know what's going to happen."

Louis could have said something, a lot, but he didn't.

"I don't know what to say to my husband. I keep thinking about it. I think, after we say the first few things, like how are you and all, then there won't be anything to say and everything will be the same again." There was a long silence as she sat there holding her drink.

Louis said, "Well, you'll have enough to talk about," thinking, Jesus — "He'll want to know all about it."

"No, he won't."

"He'll ask you things. How you were treated —"

"Uh-unh. He'll ask me how I am, he'll say well, why don't you get some rest. And put it out of his mind."

"If you feel like telling him about it," Louis said — actually giving her advice; he couldn't believe it — "then tell him."

"He won't listen. He'll be moody for a day or

so and then, it'll be like it never happened."

"Well, then grab him by the front of the shirt, say, Hey, listen, I got something to tell you."

She shook her head. "He won't listen. I know."

"Why not? I mean something happens to his wife — what's the matter with him?"

"He's an asshole," Mickey said. She heard Louis say, "Oh," but she wasn't listening to Louis; she continued to hear the word she had said out loud for the first time in her life and began wondering if she could improve on it.

"He's a pure asshole." No, "pure" didn't do anything for it. She said, "Do you know what I mean?"

"Sure," Louis said. "Unless what you really mean, he's a prick."

"He probably is at work, dealing with employes. But in life he's . . . the other." Losing her nerve again she brought it back quickly. "An asshole."

"Well —" Louis didn't know what to say. "You got a nice house, you got plenty of money —"

"You mean so be grateful? You sound like my mother. Do you have a cigarette?"

"I'll look," Louis said. He pulled himself up and walked out of the living room.

Maybe they'd get along, Mickey thought. If her mother didn't know what Louis did for a living. (What *did* he do?) Tell mom he had an important position with GM, at the Tech Center. Her mother would say, "That's nice." Her dad would say, "Oh? I had some good friends at GM belonged to the Detroit Golf Club. Where do you play, Louis?"

"I couldn't find any regular ones. How about one of these?" He was holding several joints in the palm of his hand.

"Is that what I think it is?"

"Yeah, good stuff. I think Colombian."

"I've never smoked it before."

"Colombian? It's not that different you'd taste it." He let them roll out of his hand onto the coffee table.

"Do you smoke it all the time?"

"No, once in awhile," Louis said. "Or like if I'm with somebody, a girl, you know, and we want to get a little high first."

"Do you use other drugs?"

"No hard stuff, no. Coke maybe, but not as an every week thing. Maybe if it's there, somebody offers it."

"I'd like to try the grass," Mickey said.

As Louis got up he seemed to realize what she meant. "You never smoked before?"

"Uh-unh." She watched him pick up matches from the table and light the cigarette, the twisted end flaming for a moment. As he handed it to her she said, "What do you do?"

"You smoke it."

"I mean how?"

"The way you smoke your True greens. It'll work."

"Don't you use a — what do you call it, the thing you hold the joint with?"

"A roach chip? If you're poor. No, we get plenty of grass. It gets down, throw it away and have another. But I think one'll do the job."

Mickey inhaled the cigarette. She didn't like the smell. She handed it to Louis who took a drag, handed it back and picked up their empty glasses. She noticed, watching him as he walked out of the room, he didn't exhale. She drew on the cigarette and tried holding in the smoke. When Louis came back with fresh drinks she said, a little surprised or disappointed, "I don't feel anything."

"Well, you got time," Louis said. "You don't want to go home we can always sit around and get stoned."

She said, "I don't understand. You know it? There's so goddamn much I don't understand. Do you?"

"Be happy," Louis said. "What else you want?"

"What else do *you* want?" She reached out the joint and Louis reached out a hand and she passed him the cigarette.

"Money," Louis said. "That's all."

"Ooooh no," Mickey said. "That's what everybody thinks, but money has nothing to do with happiness. What about your health?"

"Well, say I had a yacht," Louis said, "great big cruiser. See, I could sit on the fantail there and throw up and have the maid bring me an Alka-Seltzer and it would beat the shit out of laying in the weeds down on Michigan Avenue. I know a guy I went to school with, he ended up down there drinking Thunderbird, no teeth, half his stomach taken out. I was down at one of those Ethnic Festivals, you know, on the river? I think it was the Polish or the Ukrainian Festival. I see him there, filthy dirty, staggering around, I couldn't believe it. I said to myself, I'm never gonna be like that, ever."

Mickey was surprised at the way Louis let the cigarette burn as he spoke, not worrying about wasting it. She said, "He could've had money and lost it because he was drinking."

"He didn't have shit," Louis said. "He worked at Sears in automotive service, putting on the new poly-glass radials. He was *frus*trated because he didn't have any money."

"Why didn't he get another job?"

"Where?" Louis passed the cigarette to her and she kept it.

"I don't know. Where do people work? They work all over, do all kinds of things."

"You ever work?"

"Of course I worked."

"Where?"

"At Saks."

"How long?"

"Well, the last time" — the only time — "it was a little more than five weeks."

"Five *weeks?*"

"I was part-time. A flyer. Let me tell you something," Mickey said, "you talk about frustration —"

"Five *weeks* —"

"Let me tell you, okay? You think you can sit quietly and not open your mouth and listen for a change?"

"Go ahead, tell me."

"God, I left my purse there."

"Richard'll go through it, see if you got any Tampax or a diaphragm."

"I was praying all these past four days I wouldn't get the curse. I'm overdue."

"Maybe you're pregnant."

"No way. God, I hate that expression. No way. I mean there isn't any possible way I could be. Well, he can have it — God, he was awful. He smelled. I know my wallet's at home on the kitchen table, with my car keys."

"So you had this terrible frustrating job —"

"You weren't allowed to carry a purse," Mickey said. "You had to carry a Saks Fifth Avenue shopping bag so this little snip in Security could look in it if you were walking around the store or you were leaving and make sure you weren't stealing anything."

"I bet there were ways," Louis said.

"She was a little snippy snitch," Mickey said. "Fat little company snitch, with acne."

"I can see her," Louis said.

"She'd say" — Mickey effected a snippy tone " 'You have anything in that bag?' And pull it, almost pull it away from you, and look inside."

"I'd tell her to put it where the sun don't shine," Louis said.

"I'd say, 'No, I don't have anything in it. I carry it around empty, you dumb shit.' That's what I wanted to say."

"Why didn't you?"

"Why didn't I? I'd get fired."

"So, you were just working there for fun, were you?"

"I was proving something to myself."

"When was this, before you were married?"

"Last year."

"Jesus Christ, you're living in that big fucking house, you drive your Grand Prix to work —"

"It wasn't for *money,* you dumb shit. *No,* it wasn't for that at all."

"What was it for?" He got up and left.

What was it for?

To get out in the world. No, he wouldn't accept that, Saks Fifth Avenue as the world, or even as a step into it. But it was.

He came back in with two fresh drinks. She didn't remember finishing the last one.

"I still don't feel it," Mickey said, "the grass. Maybe just a teeny bit."

"A teeny weeny bit?" Louis said.

"A teeny-weeny *weeny* weeny-weeny bit," Mickey said. "What got me the most wasn't the snitch with the acne or the other salesgirls in Young Circle who'd, you'd have a customer and they'd try and steal her after you practically broke your ass showing her clothes. The woman'd say, 'Oh, now, what goes with this?' Helpless, making you think for her. Or this fat fat broad would come in, 5-feet tall weighing about 200 pounds and she'd ask for, because she's only 5 feet or about 4-11?, she'd ask for petite." A nasal sound. " 'Let me see what you have in petite.' Petite, she couldn't get a petite over her left boob. The slobs you had to wait on — they'd take a bunch of dresses and things into the booth, walk out and leave everything on the floor. But the worst, you know what the very worst was? What really got me?"

"What?" Louis said.

"These women who threw their charge plates at you."

"They threw 'em at you, huh?" Louis said.

"They'd sort of flip them." Mickey twisted sideways in the chair, raising her shoulder and gave him a backhand motion with her hand. "Like that. Like, 'I'm hot shit, I've got this Saks charge plate.' Christ, who doesn't?"

"You throw it back?"

"No, I didn't throw it back."

"Why didn't you?"

"I wanted to. God, I wanted to so bad."

"So you quit instead," Louis said.

"I couldn't stand it."

"Well see, most people," Louis said, "they don't have that choice you did. They got to stay there and take that shit, cause they don't have a big house to drive home to."

"*Nobody* has to take it," Mickey said. "It isn't worth it."

"No, you can steal a Grand Prix if you haven't got one," Louis said. "Or you can stick up supermarkets. I stuck up a liquor store one time, got $742, but it scared the shit out of me and I went back to hustling cars till I ended up in Southern Ohio Correctional. Then I did, oh, different things till I got sent to Huntsville and down there I said that's all, man, no more." He was silent a moment. "And here we are, huh?"

Very seriously, squinting at him, Mickey said, "Those are prisons?"

"They sure are. I've spent — well, it's almost a quarter of my life in one joint or another. Wayne County, Dehoco, Southern Ohio, Huntsville. I haven't been to Jackson yet and I'm not going. I promised myself that."

"What if you get caught?"

"If I have to I'll put the gun in my mouth first."

"Really?"

"Cross my heart. You got a button unbuttoned there and I can almost see your titties."

"You wouldn't see much," Mickey said, looking down as she fastened the buttons she'd missed. "Where's Huntsville?"

"Texas. I was down there, I was hanging around McAllen and Brownsville waiting for a load of grass, like about a ton of it. I was never into anything like that before, but I was doing it for a man I knew, just bringing it back, not dealing or anything. I was sitting around there in the bars listening to the radio, all that cucaracha music. You get XECR Reynosa you want to hear some rock. No good jazz at all, none."

"You like jazz?" Mickey said.

"We got some tapes, I'll play 'em," Louis said. "You like Blue Mitchell?"

"I don't know if I've heard him. Les McCann?"

"Yeah. Gil Evans?"

"I think so."

"Art Blakey and the Jazz Messengers. Or a little electronic voo-doo, Lonnie Liston Smith."

"I like Buddy Rich," Mickey said.

"Yeah, he's all right," Louis said. "I'm waiting there about two weeks in Brownsville, McAllen, finally I said fuck-it, I'm going home. But by then I didn't have any money for gas. So I said okay, I'll go out and pick melons for a few days, maybe a week. See, the only reason I was down there I was fucking desperate and this grass was gonna make it, get me a stake. So I sign up at a place, Stanzik Farms, go out and start picking and they call a strike. Actually the strike was going on and I was hired like as a scab, buck sixty an hour. We were out in the fields and the ones on strike were up on the road forming a picket line and this Chicano girl with the union would yell at us through a bullhorn. She'd yell like, *'Vengase! Para respecto, hombres!'* 'Come on, for your self-respect.' There'd be police cars there, these hotshot troopers with their sunglasses, chewing gum. Never smile. I think they teach them that at the academy. You're out there, never smile, trooper, show you're a human being, man. Some company people, a foreman, came by there in a pickup truck. Then this Chicano girl, Helen Mendez" — Louis grinned, shaking his head — "she was something, she'd start calling the names of people she knew out in the field, asking where their dignity was, using that word, *dignity,* and their respect for justice. She'd say, 'Look at your friends here on the picket line, going hungry for the sake of a just wage. You should've heard her; she was an actress. And pretty soon some of the pickers they'd be looking at each other, and you'd see them take the sacks off their shoulder and come out of the field."

"And you were one of them," Mickey said.

"Well, I wasn't making all that much and my goddamn back was killing me, that stoop work, Jesus — so I thought well, join the union. They looked like they were having a better time than we were."

"They sent you to prison for striking?"

"No, not for striking," Louis said. "See, they started running the company pickup truck up and down the road past the strikers, giving us a lot of dust and kicking up gravel. Then when the girl, Helen Mendez, would start calling names over the bullhorn, the pickup truck started playing music — see, the radio was hooked up to a speaker on the roof of the truck — blaring it out so nobody'd be able to hear her yelling their names. I remember, I even remember one of the songs was *Falling Leaves,* Christ, Roger Williams playing it. And *Who Can I Turn To.* Helen Mendez'd yell at the truck, 'Hey, you squares, get XECR Reynosa!' You want me to light another one?"

Mickey blinked. "I think I can feel it now."

"Get up and walk you'll find out."

"I'm too comfortable."

"We'd sit out there on the line, this trooper with

his ranger hat on'd come along make us get up and stand so many feet apart and so many feet from the edge of the field. We'd say, 'What the fuck do you care if we sit down?' He'd give us this mean squinty no-shit look and point his stick and say something about hauling our ass in if we gave him any mouth. He didn't say nothing to the Stanzik foreman who'd come by in the pickup seeing if he could make us jump back out of the way. I remember the radio was playing *Okie from Muskogee* — you remember it?"

"Sure," Mickey said. "Merle Haggard."

"How come you know it?"

"I've got a radio too," Mickey said. "I'm not bragging, but we've got about five and only one of them, the one in the kitchen, works."

"I'll fix 'em for you," Louis said. "I was in the Navy. I was a Radioman Third."

"And a melon-picker for half a day," Mickey said.

"Not even that," Louis said. "This truck comes along playing *Okie from Muskogee* blaring out and some of the strikers they'd hold their signs out in the road and raise them as the truck skinned by. So the foreman got pissed-off, he decided to skin us a little closer, make us jump, and the truck hit this old man, threw him about thirty feet down the road and into the ditch. I saw it, I saw the truck swerve at the man deliberately. Everybody ran over to where he was laying there with his broken leg. The trooper came over, taking his leather book out, and you know what he did?"

"What?" Mickey said.

"He gave the old man laying there a ticket for obstructing traffic."

Mickey thought of the security girl with acne at Saks Fifth Avenue.

"I asked one of the strikers if I could use his car to go into town," Louis said. "I had to get out of there, go someplace maybe have a drink. He said sure, for a dollar. I got in the car, started up the road and there was the foreman standing beside his pickup truck with the door open. I think it was the way he was standing, hand on his hip watching, not giving a shit, you know? I gunned the car at him. I just wanted to make him jump, the son of a bitch, but I cut it too close, took his door off and broke both his legs."

"God," Mickey said. "What happened?"

"Everybody cheered," Louis said. "I was arrested, charged with attempted murder, plea-bargained it down to felonious assault and got two to five in Huntsville. Served thirty months, same amount of time I was in the Navy, and I'll tell you something. Even being at Norfolk, Virginia, I liked the Navy a little better."

"I can't imagine being in prison," Mickey said.

"Don't ever go," Louis said.

He got up and came over to the La-Z-Boy. When he bent over her, his face almost touching hers, she said, "What're you doing?"

"I'm just seeing what you got."

"Get out of there!" She pushed him, mad or

pretending to be mad. Pretending.

"I thought we were friends," Louis said, straightening.

"God," Mickey said. "Do you believe it?"

"Listen, I don't have any idea what's going on," Louis said. "I think I'm high . . . and I'm starved to death." He picked up his cap and started for the door.

Mickey said, "Well, don't go away mad."

"I'm not mad, I'm hungry. I'm gonna go out and get us a pizza. You hungry?"

"I guess I am," Mickey said. "I hadn't realized it."

"The grass," Louis said. "Pizza all right, or you want something else?"

"No, that's fine." He was at the door, putting his cap on. Mickey said, "I didn't finish telling you. The day I quit Saks — no, the day before — I had a big leather purse I'd been carrying for a week at least."

Louis waited, his hand on the doorknob. "Yeah? The snippy one catches you —"

"The snippy security snitch," Mickey said, "she sees me and stops." Then, in the snippy tone, " 'You can't carry that purse.' I said, 'It's all right, don't get excited.' She said, 'You're not al*lowed* to carry a purse unless you're management personnel. Are you a department manager?' Knowing damn well I'm not. Very sweetly I said, 'No, I'm not.' She said, "Then you can't carry that purse ever again.' And I said to her, 'Oh, bullshit,' and walked out."

"You said that?" Louis said.

"Yeah, 'Oh bullshit.' "

"Well, it's a start," Louis said. "I'll be right back."

19

"Louis?"

"What?"

"I'm drinking beer and I don't even like beer."

Louis held a wedge of pizza almost to his mouth. He said, "Jesus Christ," and began shaking his head. "How'd you know my name?"

"I'm drinking it because you said you had to with pizza," Mickey said, "and you know what? It's pretty good."

"You do whatever somebody tells you?"

They were sitting on the floor eating off the coffee table, the table congested, littered with pizza, the flat carryout box, cans of Stroh's, paper napkins, two packs of Salem 100s, three joints, matches, empty glasses, full ashtrays, the box of Halloween masks, Mickey's bra. She said, "Maybe I do, you know it? That's probably the whole trouble — anything anybody says. Yeah? Well, screw 'em."

"I ask you how you know my name," Louis said, "you tell me that's the whole trouble and screw 'em."

Her mind was clear and alive. That was a long time ago he had asked about his name. About an hour ago. She said, "The fat guy, the fake policeman. He's not a real one, is he? God, I hope not."

"He told you?"

"Yeah. What's his name? No, what's the colored guy's name?"

"Christ, everybody knows everybody," Louis said. He got up and stood for a moment before carefully walking out of the room.

Mickey began to think about the fat policeman in his T-shirt, seeing him on top of her, his red face, his breathing, saying things to her. She said aloud, "Oh, my God." When Louis came back and eased himself to the floor and popped open two cans of beer, Mickey said, "I remembered something. Were you really taking me home or someplace else?"

"You said you didn't want to go."

"But were you really taking me home?"

"We were almost there, weren't we?"

"*Answer* me. Were you?"

"Yes, I was taking you home."

"You know what the fat policeman said?" Mickey closed her eyes to see him and hear the words again. "He said, 'Don't move or holler or I'll kill you right now . . . on my mother's bed —' "

"His mother used to live with him."

"*Listen* to me. He said, '. . . or I'll kill you right now on my mother's bed and . . . *not wait till after.*' "

"He said that?"
"Or, '. . . not wait till later.' After or later."
"Well, the guy's a little wacko," Louis said. "He's got a framed picture of Adolph Hitler, a swastika flag. He's got about, Christ, a hundred guns, hand grenades —"
"He was going to *kill* me," Mickey said. "He shot at us, didn't he?"
"Well, he was a little sore," Louis said. "I'm telling you, the guy's wacko."
"But you were taking me home, weren't you?" Mickey said. "No place else for anything?"
"I was taking you home," Louis said.

Mickey heard sounds, one sound over and over, a telephone ringing. She opened her eyes, lying in the reclining La-Z-Boy again. A lamp was on next to Louis' chair, the room dark beyond the yellow glow of the lampshade, the windows dark. She could hear traffic sounds outside, faintly, and the phone ringing.
"Are you going to answer it?"
"Twelve . . . thirteen . . . fourteen . . . it'll ring twenty-five times," Louis said. "That's how long he waits. Then it'll stop." But the phone stopped ringing as he said it. There was silence. "Must've been somebody else."
"What time is it?"
"About eleven. No, twenty-five after."
"I don't know what to do," Mickey said.
"Who does."
"I don't feel good."

"Seventh inning," Louis said. "Get up and stretch."

She watched him push up from the chair and wondered if that's what he was going to do, raise his arms and stretch. No, he was going somewhere, probably to the bathroom. She said to herself, You have to go home. She heard the blender working in the kitchen. Louis came back in with two foamy looking drinks. Mickey shook her head.

"Vodka collins," Louis said. "Look good to you?"

Mickey took one. "But I can't stay high forever. I have to go home."

"You get way down, you have to come all the way back," Louis said. "What happened to the party girl?"

"She's all partied out."

"Get her back up," Louis said. He went over to the hi-fi on a shelf, pushed in a cassette and brought music out of hidden speakers. Mickey looked around, but couldn't see them.

"Groove Holmes, help you get straightened out."

"I really should go."

"You already said that."

"Did I?" She was drinking the vodka collins and, yes, beginning to feel better already. She reached, got a pack of Salems from the table and lit a cigarette.

"You want a hand-rolled?"

"I'd better not."

"I should go home," Louis said, "I better not.

What do you *want* to do? Your old man's not home —"

"He might be, now."

"Bet," Louis said. "How much? He won't be home cause he's got to have time to think what to tell you, decide how to act. He's wondering if he should lie about the whole thing or what."

"*Lie* about it?"

"Tell you the girl was only working for him, something like that. See, he can bullshit you about the money thing, how he put all that away — have you believing it was for you and him. But the part about the girl he's got to get straight in his mind what he's gonna tell you, so you can't shoot any holes in it."

"I don't care if he's with a girl," Mickey said. She didn't, and it surprised her as she realized it.

"Well, he still isn't gonna be home."

She could think of Frank as "that son of a bitch," picturing him with a girl named Melanie. That was one way the offended wife might react. Or she could feel sorry for herself. But what she genuinely felt was, what? Nothing. Indifference. Did she love him? No. She didn't even particularly like him, with or without the girlfriend. And, God, that was a big one to finally admit.

But something bothered her about the time element and what Frank had been doing the last few days. Not with the girl, that didn't matter. But what had he been doing about paying the ransom?

"You like Groove? A little *Green Dolphin Street*," Louis said. "Here, gimme that." He took their empty glasses out to the kitchen.

Mickey raised the recliner and stood up, walked over to the phone in the bay of windows and looked down at it. 956-9547. She was a bit wobbly but her head was clear; she felt eighty-five per cent better than when she had awakened. Now — if Frank wasn't home, the logical thing would be to call him in Freeport, let him know she was all right. Which had nothing to do with being indifferent to him; she was being considerate. Nice. *No* — not nice. She was simply being . . . something like courteous. Because once he paid them he'd want to know if they'd released her . . . and if she wasn't home and he was calling every ten minutes to find out . . .

Louis came in with new drinks as she picked up the phone. "You calling him?"

"His answering service." Mickey dialed and waited. "Hi, this is Mrs. Dawson. Have there been any calls today? . . . I mean from Mr. Dawson . . . Oh, okay. Thank you."

Louis was still holding the drinks, looking at her. "No calls, huh?"

Mickey shook her head. She came over to Louis and took her vodka collins in both hands.

Louis stood by the TV set, holding a joint, looking at the black-and-white picture, a lab scene in a 1950s monster movie. He said, "It's got to be the right one. I'll tell you, like that *Two Thousand*

and One? When the spaceship's going through all those shapes and colors and shit? Say that fast as you can three times. The spaceship goes through shapes and shit. Go ahead."

Mickey was staring at the TV picture.

"The spaceship . . . no, the apeshit goes through space and ships," Louis said. He was grinning, weaving, as he turned off the TV — "This one isn't any good" — came over and offered Mickey the joint, stumbling against the arm of the La-Z-Boy. "Move over."

"Get away," Mickey said, "get out of here." Playing with him again? No, this time serious, annoyed. Louis went over to his chair and rolled into it, spilling some of his drink.

"Why did it take him so long?" Mickey said.

"Who?"

"You called Monday night. Three days later you say my husband's paid you. Why did it take him three days?"

"Why don't you ask him?"

"If he believes you've let me go — or else he wouldn't have paid you — why hasn't he called home to find out?"

"He's *your* husband," Louis said. "I told you before what I thought."

"It's the three days he waited," Mickey said. "Why?" She thought, To see what would happen if he *didn't* pay?

Louis said, "Listen, if he doesn't love you anymore I'll take care of you."

"You called him again Wednesday — I was *sit-*

ting there — but you didn't talk to him. Someone else answered. The girl? Melanie?" The name sounded funny to her, strange, saying it. Her husband's girlfriend. "But she wouldn't let you talk to him. So the other one, the black guy, went down to Freeport, didn't he? Because I didn't hear him for two days." Mickey stopped, realizing something. "You two are the ones who thought it up, right? Because you're the ones who did it. You were using the fat policeman to help out. Isn't that right? But you and the black guy are the main ones, you're partners. The way you spoke to each other in my house —"

She thought about it some more while Louis smoked the joint. It was interesting watching her. She was a cute looking lady sitting there, riled up but calm, different than the lady who'd been in Richard's mother's room.

"The black guy went to Freeport and supposedly contacted my husband and got the money. Where is he?"

"He just called this afternoon," Louis said. "He hasn't had time to be *any*where."

"He called," Mickey said, "but you didn't talk to him, did you? I asked you if my husband had paid and you said, 'I guess so.' Something like that. I could tell you weren't sure, and you were a little upset, mad. Were you there when he called?"

"I was there as long as you were."

"Then why didn't he talk to *you?* If you and he are partners."

"That's a good question," Louis said. He sat up a little, wondering if maybe he could learn something if he paid attention. Give her a little bit and let her chew on it, but not too much.

She said, "You're not absolutely sure your partner was paid, are you? God, a million dollars."

"Nobody's abso*lute*ly sure of anything," Louis said.

"But you have a feeling, don't you? Something's going on and you don't know what."

"I'll tell you," Louis said, "the whole thing's getting pretty weird, you want to stop and think about it."

"For all you know, he didn't even see my husband," Mickey said. "What did he say on the phone?"

"He said it was all set and to take you home."

"That's what the fat policeman told you he said. It's all set. What else?"

"It's all set . . . he's got the money and take you home."

"He said he had *all* the money? A million dollars?"

"He said he had the money, yeah."

"You mean the fat policeman said it."

"Yeah, Richard said it. I told you I didn't talk to him."

She hesitated and said the name to herself, Richard. Then to Louis, "You were in the house, but your buddy spoke to Richard instead of you. The fat policeman's name is Richard?"

Louis shook his head, tired. "That's right."

"Why didn't he call you to the phone?"

"Maybe I was in the bathroom."

"Were you?"

"No, I was upstairs. I was looking at his gun collection. Matter of fact I was looking at a book of his, *Death Investigation.* The son of a bitch is really weird."

"I'm only asking," Mickey said, "but isn't it strange he'd tell Richard and not you? After you planned the whole thing together?"

"We didn't plan it together. It was his idea."

"But you're equal partners?"

"Yeah."

"Maybe you're not, Louis." Mickey sipped her drink, reached over to place it on the coffee table and got a cigarette. "Maybe you only think you are."

"It entered my head," Louis said. "You look around, I'll tell you, you're not sure who's side anybody's on."

"Louis?"

He wasn't looking at her; he was thinking.

"Louis, tell me something."

"What?"

"What's your partner's name?"

"What difference does it make?"

"Come on, you big poop. Tell me."

"His name's Ordell Robbie, but that's not gonna do you any good."

"How does he know my husband?"

"He doesn't *know* him. He sold him a lot of building materials and things, appliances, Ordell had ripped off different places, and then'd sell to your husband cheap," Louis said. "See, that's another thing. You start talking and you can get your husband in all kinds of deep shit, and where does that get you? Right?"

"There's nobody I'd care to tell," Mickey said. "*I'm* not your problem anymore, Louis." She got up out of the recliner, remembering him referring to the seventh inning; it seemed like yesterday. She stretched and yawned and blinked her eyes and felt pretty good, considering everything.

"Is that Woodward out there?"

Louis nodded. "Half block down the street."

"Lend me about ten bucks for a cab," Mickey said, "and I'll go home."

"I'll take you, I told you I would."

"No, stay where you are. I appreciate the offer though."

"You can't stand over there on the corner waiting for a cab," Louis said, "Woodward and Six Mile, it's loaded with whores. Some guy's liable to come along, try and pick you up."

"He'd better not," Mickey the ballbuster said.

20

There was a 12th Precinct patrolman by the name of Randy Dixson — an energetic young guy three years with the Detroit Police Department, a part-time tree-trimmer — who had been working Vice the past several months and going out of his mind: hanging around Menjoe's watching the guys dancing with each other; hanging around toilets waiting for some poor guy to reach for a cop's yang by mistake; sick to death of that summer-night whore beat, hassling the crazy ladies and getting his shoes scuffed and stepped on each evening by eighty-five pairs of white plastic boots; the clean-up-the-neighborhood pickets blaming, belittling him, calling him terrible names, whore-sucker on the take . . . he was beginning to think, Enough of this shit, quit and trim trees full time for a living. It was in his mind, sitting outside the Coney Island and chatting with some of the ladies when the backup call came squawking out of the radio, *Officer in need of assistance,* a mile-and-a-half north, hang a right to 1035 State Fair, the radio calling and calling all the way there, and the radio was right, it was an event.

Before it was over there were TV news vans and mini-cameras on the scene, the street blocked with barricades and a good crowd over at the Fairgrounds watching through the fence.

There was a shot-up police car in front of the residence, a patch of blood in the street, a critically wounded police officer with a sucking chest wound on his way to Detroit General; armed police officers behind blue-and-white cruisers and a heavy-duty Tactical Mobile Unit squad with flak jackets, rifles, shotguns and gas grenades.

Randy Dixson showed up in his light poplin jacket covering a .357 Mag beneath his left arm; squinted at the scene chewing his gum; learned that some crazy fucker was in there with automatic weapons, guy used to be a rent-a-cop, first reported to be wearing a T-shirt and armed with a revolver, but now wearing, it looked like, some kind of uniform and moving from window to window firing all kinds of weapons at them. They'd glimpse him as he'd yell something and then fire his weapon and they'd return fire, blowing out his windows, all except the ones on the second floor that looked like they'd been boarded up, like the guy had been preparing for a shoot-out. He kept yelling something about "fury" or "furor." It didn't make sense, sounding like he was crying; but when they'd try to talk him out with a bullhorn, he'd rip at them with his machine gun. Crazy fucker, you couldn't talk to him.

They put Randy Dixson on the porch of the house next door to the left. He could edge his face past the corner and see the side door of 1035. A couple of TMU guys with riot guns were there pressed against the house, looking like they were about to go in. But after a few minutes, looking toward the street, nodding and giving hand-signals back, they moved away from the house. Randy Dixson kept looking at that side entrance to 1035.

He watched it until he decided fuck it, it was citation time; he'd rather fight crime than Dutch-elm disease and went over the porch rail, across the drive and in through the side door. (Why hadn't the TMU guys just *done* it?) Randy Dixson stood in the short hallway looking into the living room that was all blown to shit, rubble. The cop-shooter was near the front windows, crouched behind a maroon couch, lifting his head to see out without being seen. Young Randy had him, saw in his mind the Medical Examiner's report describing exit wounds in the guy's chest, said, "Hey!" loud, and put three .357s into Richard Edgar Monk dead-center as the swastika arm came swinging around with a burp gun.

Mickey opened the front door Friday morning, picked up the *Free Press* from the stoop and saw Richard smiling at her from the picture, Richard standing in his T-shirt by a birdbath, the statue of the Virgin Mary looking over his shoulder. The headline read

NAZI CULTIST KILLED
IN GUN BATTLE WITH POLICE

Mickey stood barefoot in the kitchen with her coffee and the *Free Press*, as she did every morning, and read about Richard Edgar Monk, cultist, racist, anti-Communist, ex-private security guard. *Cultist.* She didn't think of Richard as a cultist, she thought of him as a frightening but unsuccessful rapist. She read about his gun collection, Nazi flag, photographs, war memorabilia.

She read about a woman's purse (the same one she had carried to work her last week at Saks) found in the upstairs bedroom, cold cabbage on the stove, dishes in the kitchen sink, as though several people had been recently living in the house.

She read about the siege and about Richard with interest, though quite calmly, with a feeling she identified as relief. Richard was dead. Louis wouldn't hurt her. She wondered if Louis had seen the paper. Probably not. She bet Louis would sleep late; maybe he'd see it on the TV news later, maybe not.

She thought of calling Louis and telling him. Nine-five-six, nine-five-four-seven. She remembered the number. She was quite sure she remembered everything they had talked about. Louis, Richard, Ordell Robbie. Melanie . . . Frank. Frank and Melanie. She saw Frank in lime-green paisley, his golf tan, his hands in tight pockets, elbows sticking out, cool-serious Frank entering the casino with his girlfriend. The big jerk. Old enough to be her father probably. Melanie thin, but with big boobs, overdressed, lots of fake jewelry, rings. Melanie looking at him worshipfully, listening to a replay of his golf round. Melanie would have to be pretty dumb and impressionable.

Mickey had remembered to take a pack of Salem from the cluttered pizza-beer coffee table and had forgotten to take her bra. Louis could have it.

She still didn't have one on beneath a loose cotton top and it felt good. It was good to feel clean again. She'd decide later what to do about Frank's closet, if anything. She lit a Salem, went to the wall phone and without hesitating or getting words ready, dialed the number in Freeport.

A girl's voice answered.

Mickey said, "Melanie?" and was surprised at the quiet, even tone.

The voice said, "Yeah?"

"This is Mrs. Dawson," Mickey said.

"Oh, hi."

Mickey hesitated, stopped for a moment. "Is . . . Frank there?"

"No, he's out. I think he had to go to a meeting."

"With the Japanese?"

"I don't know who he's with, some business guys. Hold on a minute, will you?"

Mickey waited, feeling heat rise up into her face. She waited what seemed to be several minutes.

"Hi, I'm back. Any message?"

"Would you have him call me at home?"

"Sure. Bye."

Mickey replaced the phone, her hand shaking. She had believed she was ready to talk to Frank — with an even, normal tone, on an adult level — and listen quietly, unmoved, while the son of a bitch tried to explain what he'd been doing the past four days. And she had handled herself adequately just now, considering it was the first time she had ever spoken to a known girlfriend, each aware of the other's role. She'd handled it without preparation, without knowing it was going to happen. But she hadn't been anywhere near as poised or offhand as the girlfriend. It scared her.

It also made her mad. If she wasn't ready yet to take on Frank and his girlfriend then she'd *get* ready. Not by memorizing things to say, faking it, but by keeping a hard straight edge on her thinking. By keeping emotions in their place. By forgetting roles she might play and simply being herself. If she could.

Louis had gone to sleep in the recliner. He woke up at three-thirty and went to bed. He woke up again at ten, Friday morning, not feeling too red hot but passable. He had two ice-cold cans of Stroh's and a can of hot chili and felt a world better. What he ought to have done then was clean up the place, but decided the hell with it. He wasn't going to hang around here and think and wait for the phone to ring. Ordell would get back when he got back. Or, he wouldn't get back. There wasn't anything Louis could do about that; so he decided he'd call his sister in Allen Park and go visit her.

It was his older sister, Louise. Three years older. She was glad to see him, kissed him and was very nice to him, hoping he'd stay awhile. His brother-in-law, Chuck, was a boring-mill operator at Ford Rouge, which Louis thought was perfect since Chuck was the most boring fucking guy he'd ever met in his life. He came home from work and asked Louis if he was staying out of jail and made a few other remarks, like maybe Louis could get a good job busting rocks, with all his experience. Louis was polite in return, courteous, drinking the man's beer, and kept himself from breaking Chuck's jaw. His brother-in-law didn't get the morning paper; he left for work too early to read it and didn't give a shit if anybody else might want to.

So Louis didn't learn about poor Richard Edgar Monk until the six o'clock TV news came on with its mini-camera coverage. He watched it while his brother-in-law told him all about their new UAW contract. Then, when it was over, his brother-in-law said, "What was that all about?"

Ordell looked down and saw half of Richard's face in the lobby of the King's Inn, about four o'clock Friday afternoon.

It was Richard's picture on the front page of the *Detroit News*, the page folded once and lying on a set of rose-colored matched luggage, three pieces and golf clubs.

Ordell had been eying the luggage and the man it belonged to with the just-arrived Detroit Dental

Association group, because the man was about Ordell's size, a dentist who was in shape and looked to be living clean. Ordell had already decided the middle-size bag, because the big one would be full of the man's fat wife's outfits. But when he walked over to it, there was Richard looking at him, Richard in his rent-a-cop uniform giving the readers his serious no-shit look. Ordell walked off with the newspaper, took it into the cocktail lounge and had a big rum drink while he read the story, not seeing any mention of Louis or the woman. Ordell leaned back in the bar stool, said, "Lovely," and meant it, feeling like he'd just stepped out of the way of a truck coming to run him down.

No wonder nobody'd answered the phone.

He left his big rum drink, went out to the lobby and phoned Detroit, his apartment. Still no answer. Three times he'd called last night and no answer. Something was happening he'd have to find out about. One thing for sure though, Richard had not killed the woman.

What had he been thinking that he could call Richard up and tell Richard to kill a person like that with a gun? He'd told himself well, he wasn't doing it, Richard was. The trick then would be to keep from thinking about it, put it out of his mind in Paris, France, with $150,000, push it way away. Except he'd seen a man killed one time, shot dead. He'd had nothing to do with it, it was a crazy insane motherfucker name of Bobby Lear who'd stuck his piece in the man's car window and shot the man two three times while the man's little boy about 3 years old sat on the seat with his big eyes wide open. Then somebody later on had shot Bobby Lear in the Montclair Hotel and that was fine, helping to make the streets safe again. But seeing somebody shot in real life was not anything like seeing them shot in the movies. That business with the .38 Smiths? Saying to Louis nobody was gonna stand in his way if it meant going to Jackson? That was two kids saying how far they could spit. Back on the stool with his rum drink, Ordell said to himself, Could you see it, pulling a trigger on the woman, really for true? Then how come he'd thought it was all right for Richard to pull the trigger?

Something had been wrong with his head after talking to the tall chick he should've left in the ocean. That would've been different and not too hard to do with the tall chick. But he wouldn't have to've done that either. He just had to think of another idea. Or go back to the original million-dollar idea and not let the tall chick mess up his mind. Tell her, Hey, shit, I'm doing it. Bug the fuck off. She was something though — my. He went out to the phone in the lobby again and called her at Fairway Manor.

"What's happening?"

"Just a sec."

She always was saying just a sec when he called and would be gone before he could stop her.

"Wanted to see if he's awake yet," Melanie said. "He's been in the bag for two days now, drinking and taking little nappies."

"His wife —" Ordell said, "Nothing happened to her."

"I know. She called this morning," Melanie said, "How come?"

"You talk to her — she's home?"

"If you don't know that," Melanie said, "I think I've got the wrong party. What happened?"

"The man was supposed to do it's no longer with us," Ordell said. "But listen to me. I want to talk to you, get a few things straightened out."

"What I don't understand," Melanie said, "if she's home, how come you're still here?"

"I'm saying to you I want to *talk*."

"Okay, we will." Very laid-back, no problem. "But not right now, okay? This guy's like a fucking yoyo. Up, he keeps telling me what a dynamite success he is, how much money he's making all the time. Then he dives and takes a guilt trip for awhile. I've got to get his head on straight and then I'll be in touch. Okay?"

"You want him straightened," Ordell said, "I'll hold him over the balcony by his feet, straighten him some. I can hold you off it too, girl, or we can go out in the boat. Call Cedric to come in from the airport where he's sitting. You understand what I'm saying?"

"Hey, Ordell?" Melanie said. "I love you when you're pissed off, but don't get so hot-blooded, okay? Let me work something out and I'll come over and see you later." Melanie paused and said quietly, "Ordell?"

"What?"

"You ever do it Florentine style?"

Frank lay in bed as though wounded, staring, the sheet twisted about his lower body, a leg exposed, arms lifeless at his sides. He was thinking that if there *were* Japanese investors would they bring their clubs or would he have to get clubs for them. Little short ones. But where? No, first, the question was, did they play golf? And Frank decided they must, if they had money. He'd speak to what's his name at the New Providence Bank about potential investors in a big condominium project. Maybe Canadians. He really would, he'd talk to the guy this afternoon. Except it was too late. And tomorrow was Saturday. He began to stir, moving his hands to his chest, raising the knee of the exposed leg. He wanted to be *doing* something. And began thinking about his Grandview condominium project in Detroit, in Sterling Heights, really. He'd better get back. He could stay here until Sunday, but he couldn't remain in this goddamn apartment any longer or in the house where he'd stayed yesterday, alone, pacing the floor, looking out at the scrub and imported palm trees. He had to get back, go to work. Settle something. Face it. *Do* it. You're goddamn right. He sucked his stomach in, running one hand through his chest hair. He didn't get where he was putting off making decisions. Fucking-A right. He kicked at the sheet, hard, to straighten it. Mickey was home, so they must've let her go; she obviously hadn't *escaped*. She was home. He'd see her, he'd tell her exactly what he wanted to tell her and no more. He'd handle it.

The other problem, the extortionists — he'd talk to Ray Shelby, see who could possibly have known anything, like some guy who might've worked for him and was fired. A colored guy. Christ, there were all kinds of colored guys working for him.

Melanie was peeking in at him. "You awake?"

"I'm going home," Frank said.

"You mean *home* home?" She came over and sat on the edge of the bed, getting a warm expression in her eyes, ready to smile or look sad.

"I've got to go back, I've got a business to run."

"Did the phone wake you?"

"No" — eyes opening with alarm, ruining his determined look — "who was it, Mickey?"

"It was the black guy again. You sure you don't know him?"

"What'd he say?"

"I don't think his heart's in it anymore. He tried another sort of half-assed threat and I said hey, hold it there, sport. You'd call the feds on Mr. Dawson with a *kid*napping charge hanging over you? Bullshit."

"How much does he want?"

"He's down to $150,000. I asked him how he'd arrived at that, a hundred and fifty. You know, why not a hundred and sixty, that's 10 grand more. He mumbled something."

"If I knew who it was —" Frank said.

"Well, it's up to you, but I know what I'd tell him. I mean after all, you *know* it's a bluff. They've already let your wife go, I think because they're scared shitless. They got into something over their head. This guy probably got high on something and decided to come in with a discount offer, you know? Like one last try."

"Did he say he'd call back or what?"

"No, he doesn't know what he's doing," Melanie paused. She said, "Frank, you're an awful lot smarter than I am, but if you want a suggestion —"

"What?" Frank reached over and took his girlfriend's hand. "Tell me."

"I'd go home," Melanie said, "and act as though the whole thing never happened, if you're worried about your wife I mean. If I were you, I suppose I would be too."

"Come here," Frank said, reaching for her. "Lie down with me, Mel."

Mel. She hated to be called Mel. But she curled up next to him, putting her hand on his chest and giving him some breast against his bare skin. Very softly she said, "I've been so worried about you, Frank. I just want it to be over." Her hand moved down from his chest, down over the mound of his stomach. After a moment she heard him suck in his breath and let it out slowly. "Do you like that?" Still softly. "All I want to do is make you happy, Frank."

He murmured something about how they would be together for a long long time.

Ordell said, "That's the Florentine, huh? What

else you got? . . . Hey, where you going? He lay back on the pillows against the headboard and had to wait for her to go to the bathroom. When she came out he said, "You sure a fine big girl."

"Thank you," Melanie said. She stood looking at him, hands on her hips, thoughtful. "We've got a minor problem. Well, actually we've got some good news and some sorta not so good news."

"Yeah, I had a feeling you had some kind of news," Ordell said. He put his hands behind his head, waiting there at ease for her to tell him.

Melanie walked over to her shirt and cut-off jeans lying on the imitation-Swedish hotel chair. "He's leaving tomorrow, going home." She stepped into the cut-offs, pulled them tight over her can, wiggling her hips, and zipped up. She said, "Ouch," and made a face. "I'm always catching my pubes."

Ordell was patient, with a mild expression in the flat light of the room. "Is that the not so good news?"

"It's not *bad* really, is it?" Melanie said. "His story is, he has to see his wife now, make an appearance, and get back to his business." She stood facing Ordell in pants but no top. "And, he wants me to come to Detroit. Which is fine, right? I'll be able to stick fairly close to him and report in. But it does fuck up getting anything settled right away. I mean while we're here."

"Wants you to go with him," Ordell said, "to his home?"

"No, I'm not actually going with him, on the

same flight or anything. He just wants me to come to Detroit for a few days. Probably stay in a motel."

"Be around, hold his hand."

"That's what it sounds like. See, he stares at the wall a lot. I'm telling him things, stroking him, trying to brainwash him around a little, and it's like trying to give him ideas with an eye-dropper."

"You going to Detroit," Ordell said, "was that your idea or his?"

"Well, I didn't come right out and suggest it. I reminded him sorta I'm the only one around he has if he wants to talk about it; the sympathetic listener. See, we don't want him to get away completely. But here's the good news. You ready?"

"I can't wait," Ordell said.

"Okay, I think what's in his head, because of the guilt trip and what's happened and everything, he wants to go back to his wife and call off the divorce."

"He say that?"

"Not in so many words. What I'm getting at, if he wants her back then he obviously doesn't want her dead. Right?"

"That's the good news," Ordell said.

"Yeah." Melanie seemed disappointed or surprised, a little pouty. "Well, the bad isn't that bad and the good isn't exactly sensational. But what it does, it gets things back to normal. I mean the money's still there, but the panic's over. Now you'll have time to set it up and do it right."

Ordell waited. He watched her put on her shirt

without unbuttoning it, slipping it over her head, and the smile for him as her face appeared. The big girl was a show.

Tying the shirttails in front, she said, "You're a hunk, Ordell, but from what I've seen you're a piss-poor extortionist, if you don't mind my saying. Think about it. You've got hubby back home with little Mickey. So what do you do? You start over. And this time maybe I can help you."

"If hubby's back home with little Mickey," Ordell said, "where's little Melanie?"

"Little Melanie's around," Melanie said. "He's still got the hots, but he's also got the guilts, and that's not something we can rush. I was thinking I might even go home for awhile and see my folks, since it's been, God, almost two years."

"Take our time," Ordell said, "and have you on the inside so to speak. Help us set the man up, huh?"

Melanie nodded. "After he gets past his worries, quits looking over his shoulder. All that money'll still be sitting there. So what's the rush?"

"You giving *me* the rush," Ordell said, "but it's a kick, you know it? Seeing a mind working above those big tits."

"Scout's honor," Melanie said. "If there's something that bothers you, hey, then let's discuss it."

"Bothers me you staying in a motel up there all by yourself. We got to do something about that," Ordell said. He gave her a nice smile. "I'll tell you something. You're a fine big girl, Mel'nie, but if you didn't have a pussy there'd be a bounty on you."

21

Mickey stayed in the house all day Friday. She wasn't ready to go out, so told herself there was a lot to do. Dust. Do the kitchen floor. Rub out the stains on the oriental in the bedroom, though they were barely noticeable. The closet — she looked in, stooped to pick up the suits on the floor, abruptly changed her mind and closed the splintered door with the hole in it. It was Frank's closet, let him take care of it. If he ever decided to come home. There was no word from him all day Friday and she made her mind up she would not call him again.

She thought about lawyers. The only ones she knew belonged to the club and were friends of both of them and played golf with Frank. That probably didn't matter, but if she had to she'd get a name out of the Yellow Pages. What she wanted wouldn't require high-priced legal assistance or a formidable name. She thought. Though at this point she didn't know the least thing about getting a divorce. She had not yet said the word aloud and just barely heard it in her mind.

She wasn't sure if she should tell Bo first. Or file and let Frank tell him, the *dad*. Or both tell him. She pictured Bo sitting in the den listening to them and finally saying, "Yeah, okay. Well, listen, I gotta go."

She didn't tell her mother the plan. When she called during the morning she *listened* to her mother: Bo was having a wonderful time but didn't say much about the tennis camp. He didn't say much about anything, did he? Getting him to talk, you had to drag it out of him. He'd come home, eat dinner and go out again to meet some of his friends, all nice polite boys. Her dad had just left to take the Cadillac in to have the oil changed and the tires rotated; it was too bad Mickey hadn't called a little sooner. Her mother didn't ask her how she was or what she'd been doing all week, though she told Mickey she hadn't gotten a letter from her in quite awhile.

It was strange, listening to her mother and seeing Louis and Richard Edgar Monk in her mind and not saying, "You should've seen Richard, mom, Richard in his sagging Jockey shorts before I kicked him in the balls. Tell dad when he gets back from watching grease jobs I got drunk and stoned with an ex-convict who's been to Huntsville and Southern Ohio something or other." Knowing all that and not saying anything about it. And her mother, half-listening, thinking about something else or not accepting what she was hearing would say — What would she say?

Saturday morning she went to the A&P and

thought about going to the club. But at eleven she was in back lying in the sun in her bathing suit, the patio door open so she could hear the phone. It didn't ring. The sun felt good at first. She wanted to fall asleep in it and wake up in shade. But then it was too hot in the closeness of the backyard. There was no air stirring. A wasp was attracted to her and she kept swiping at it with the *Saturday Review*, missing. Frank used *Forbes* and killed them instantly.

Lying in the hot sun she said, If you want to go to the club, why don't you?

She didn't want to go because it was the club; she wanted to go in order to say, Look, I'm still here. And maybe to prove something. There were still uncertainties to cope with. The new Mickey was free, but she wasn't yet that used to the idea.

They waved her over to have a Bloody and she was thinking, going into the grillroom, You might be wrong, you know. It might be you and not them at all.

Tyra Taylor said, "Hi, celeb. Sit with us and have one."

It stopped her and she almost said she was going in to change and lie on the beach; but she was being open and herself and she *could* be wrong, so she said, "Fine, I'd love to." Sat down and waited for someone to ask her how she'd been and what she'd been doing.

No one asked.

Tyra told them about her maid's car problems.

Ginny told them why she was taking Bitsy out of ballet.

Barb told them why Jackie never ate corn on the cob.

Patty told them why she was going to tell off Bank-Americard.

Ginny told them why she was going to tell off Bitsy's math teacher.

Tyra told them about Ingrid's sore bummy.

Barb told them what Chrissie liked for breakfast.

Mickey told them she'd been kidnapped.

Ginny smiled and sort of laughed; otherwise there was no response. There was no direct response to anything that was told; though when Barb said Chrissie liked Cheerios, Ginny said Bitsy liked Fruit Loops.

Then Barb, Ginny and Patty said, pretty much at the same time, that Chrissie, Bitsy and Timmie liked fried eggs, scrambled eggs, no eggs at all.

The new Mickey sat and listened for an hour and a half.

Tyra said Marshall loved her new baby dolls, one green, one apricot, with matching bikini panties.

The new Mickey tried to think of things to say but couldn't. Finally she said well, bye, and got out of there. It wasn't their fault, it wasn't her fault. It wasn't even a matter of fault.

Marshall Taylor was crossing the road from the golf course to the parking lot. Big Marsh, with his golf cap sitting on top of his head, clicking across the asphalt in his golf shoes. Big Stoop.

Mickey was between her Grand Prix and the car parked next to it. He might not see her. She watched, holding the door handle. He would go by and it would be a lot easier, not having to think up things to say. But the new Mickey said, Why would you want to do that?

"Marshall?"

As he stopped and turned his head, she saw the instant dumb expression. Think fast, Marsh. The expression changing then: a squint, mouth open, desperately trying to find a pose and words to go with it.

"Mickey? Hey, is that you?" Stalling. His gaze shifted quickly over the rows of cars — no one around — and he pulled on the peak of the golf cap. The hand reached out to her as he came in between the cars. "My God, Mickey, how are you?"

"Do you really want to know?"

"I've been worried sick about you." Frowning, perplexed, innocent, "Mick, what happened?"

"Did you try to find out?" Mickey said.

"What do you mean, when I didn't hear anything? Of course I did, I called your house. I called . . . other places. I've been looking all over for you."

"Did you call the police?"

"It was the first thing in my mind. But then I thought, Wait a minute. If you're all right — see, I thought *you* called the police, or you ran out of the house to a neighbor's. So I got out of there. Then when I didn't hear anything I thought you'd probably gone to Florida to be with Bo, meet Frank, and I didn't want to turn in a false alarm and cause you any more additional trouble, if you know what I mean."

"No, I don't," Mickey said. "What do you mean?"

"I mean anybody finding out about, well, you and I."

"Marshall, there's a hole in the closet door. There's blood all over Frank's suits."

"Jesus, I know —"

"How's your head?"

"I had to have twelve stitches." He took his golf cap off and lowered his head to show her the strip of bandage where his hairline had been shaved back a couple of inches. He said, "Maybe if we hurry up and get the door fixed —"

"What'd you tell Tyra, you were in an accident?"

"Yeah. How'd you know?"

"She says you love her new baby dolls."

"Really, you see any way we can have that door fixed before he gets home? The suits, we can take 'em in for one-day service."

"Marshall, where do you think I've been all week?"

"I don't *know,*" Marshall said. "That's what I've been so worried about. What if I came over right now and got the suits? Except I'm meeting a guy from Diesel —" He was thoughtful. "See if I can get a carpenter —" Then shook his head, "No,

I think you're gonna need a new door. Okay, I'll send somebody over to measure it, he'll *take* the door. That's better yet, then get the new one put in probably Monday or Tuesday. When's Frank get back?"

"I haven't heard," Mickey said.

"If we can have it put in before — then it'll have to be painted, won't it? The suits're no problem, but the door — How about, he sees it's gone, tell him you ran into it with something?"

"The car," Mickey said.

"I was thinking like the vacuum cleaner; you put a dent in it. Or you spilled some kind of chemical on it that had to be removed."

"Martinis," Mickey said.

"No, the door was warped and wouldn't close properly. So they had to take it. How does that sound?"

"It sounds great," Mickey said. She opened the car door and got in. Marshall stooped, the peak of his golf cap touching the window, saying something. Mickey rolled the window down.

"What?"

"I said why don't you take care of the suits and I'll call the guy about the door?" Marshall looked at his wristwatch.

"Or why don't you and Frank handle it?" Mickey said. She started the car.

"Wait a minute — *Frank?*"

"It's his closet, Marshall, and you messed it up. I'd say whatever you want to do, it's up to you and Frank." She drove off.

On the way home Mickey was thinking, If you lined them all up in their Saturday night summer outfits, how would you tell them apart?

Six days ago lying in bed she had tried to imagine who, of all the men at the club, she wouldn't mind having an affair with. And had decided — none of them.

How about, which one could she be married to? And thought, What difference would it make? They're interchangeable. If you lined them up and tried to pick a winner, it would be very easy to end up with another Frank or a Marshall. One a crook, the other a tinhorn. Or you might get a drunk or a lunch-caller or a bore, or all three. And if that was cynical or smart-ass, tough. She could revise her thinking some other time.

So if she didn't fit in, if she was uncomfortable as she tried like hell to fit, and if she got tired listening and wasn't any good at thinking up small talk, why bother?

She wasn't going home mad. Nor was it an urge to find a hobby or do something *meaningful.* She didn't plan on going to Central Africa with the Peace Corps or even to the Inner City with the Junior League. She didn't know where she was going; though a few days at Gratiot Beach would be nice. She had the key. Look in her grandmother's room — where her grandmother had died two summers ago — and see if it did look like the bedroom in Richard's house. It would be good to get off by herself. Sit on the beach and watch the freighters and ore carriers go by, the way they used to watch the ships when she was little, looking through binoculars and seeing who could identify the flag or the company insignia on the stack.

Sit and not think for a few days. Read. She missed reading. Or try writing something. "How I Was Kidnapped and Found Happiness" by Margaret Bradley Dawson. In the October *Reader's Digest*. Noodle and biscuit recipes for *Family Circle*. Or for *Cosmopolitan*, "I Rapped With My Husband's Mistress."

She wondered if there had been others before Melanie. She imagined Frank coming in with the towel, hair combed, teeth brushed, then the two of them in bed. She wondered what they said to each other in bed. She wondered what Melanie looked like; how old she was.

She remembered thinking, at Richard's house, that she didn't know her husband. But that was wrong. She had waited at least a dozen years for an individual to come out from beneath the Frank Dawson Big Dealer image. And what had finally come to light was essentially more of the same big-deal baloney, the self-importance, the trophy-winning (Melanie was a trophy), the serious business poses, the "in" attire, everything but a pinky ring. Maybe in the Bahamas he wore a shark's tooth and Melanie played with it.

Fifteen years ago her mother had said simply, "You're so lucky." Her dad had said, "That young man has a head on his shoulders." Her mother had said, "Oh, I hope, I hope —" He was nice looking; he was neat; he was a business major; number three man on the University of Michigan golf team; he was a Catholic. What else? He was a Young Republican. He belonged to the Jaycees, Rotary, Knights of Columbus. He read books on personal achievement in business, the stock market and real estate. He vowed his wife would never have to work. And so they had picked out their china and bought furniture (direct from the plant in Grand Rapids at a fifty per cent savings) because it was time to get married and everyone else was doing it.

Did she love him then? Yes. Or did she feel she *should* love him? Everyone probably had a few doubts, misgivings. The first few times he was away on business she missed him and said, Ah, good. Then what happened? Nothing. That was the trouble. What had she contributed to the marriage? Not much. Why not? Well, she had wanted to; but all Frank seemed to need was a good wife. And that wasn't being cynical or smart-ass. She should've known.

She should've said to her dad, "For Christ sake, so he's good at business —" She should've known the moment she said to Frank, smiling a little, getting ready to giggle, "My dad says you've got a head on your shoulders." And Frank, eyebrows raised slightly, had shrugged, accepting it. She *did* know. But she sold out, covered the smile and was contrite. What was so funny? What did a skinny little girl with hardly any breasts know about the seriousness of business? That was her mistake right there, selling out and accepting Frank's blueprinted view of the world.

Why had he married her? Because he *knew* she'd always back off from a disagreement. No, he wasn't that perceptive. He never sensed what was in her head or was even curious about what she thought. He married her because she qualified, just as he did, and if marriage became monotonous that's the way it was; there were plenty of things to do to keep busy.

See? He missed the point. It wasn't a question of keeping *busy* or having "nice things."

Her mother said that. "My, aren't you lucky? You have such nice things." Her dad said, "How's my princess?" Bo said, "Why do we have to eat this casserole junk all the time?" Frank said, "Why don't you get interested in something, for Christ sake, like all the other wives."

All that kind of stuff, you could grin and nudge somebody or you could take it seriously. Frank didn't know that.

Mickey turned into the drive, eased past the hedge and stopped abruptly in the backyard. Frank's Mark V was parked in front of the garage door, the trunk lid open.

22

He said, "Are you all right?"

"Yes, I'm fine. How're you?" Like two strangers. Mickey dropped her purse and keys on the breakfast table. Frank answered her, stooping at the counter to get something from the lower cupboard, but she didn't hear him clearly. The trip went well, or it was hell, something like that. He came up with a bottle of vodka. There was a tray of ice on the counter, tonic water, a lime, an iced-tea spoon and a paring knife.

"You want a drink?"

"Fine," Mickey said. "When did you get back?" Wondering who would finally break it open.

"I just walked in. Oh, you mean the flight? I got in at 11:45; it was twenty minutes late. Then I stopped by the office on the way."

"Did you see Bo?"

"On the way back, no, I didn't have time. We've got a few more problems on the Grandview job. All the sod was supposed to be in a month ago? They're not half finished. I come back, none of the landscaping's done."

"Or would you rather talk about golf?" Mickey said.

Frank stared at her, for a moment curious. "You asked me why I didn't see Bo, I'm telling you. Because I've got nothing to do outside of getting a hundred goddamn units sold before the end of the summer and I didn't have time down there to play any golf."

Or else he would have told her about it. She said nothing and used the silence, letting it settle, as Frank began to cut lime wedges with the paring knife. Now:

"Did you pay them?"

Frank glanced at her, the knife still for a moment. "No, I didn't have to. They backed off."

"When did they back off?"

"*When?* When I wouldn't pay them. They were trying to pull something and they were in way over their heads." He was squeezing the lime wedges, dropping them in the glasses. "It was a bluff and I called it, that's all."

"What if they weren't bluffing?" Mickey said.

"But they were." He was stirring the drinks now with the iced-tea spoon, concentrating, as though so many stirs were required and he was counting them. "I could see there wasn't anything to worry about."

Mickey reached across with her left hand and swept the drinks from the counter. They struck the base of the wall by the telephone, exploding in a burst of glass, liquid and ice, but Mickey didn't see this. She was watching Frank and saw his head snap up and his eyes open in a startled expression she had never seen before.

She said, "What if they weren't bluffing, Frank?"

"Christ, what's the matter with you?"

"Answer me, goddamn it!"

He seemed concerned with broken glass — glancing over at the wall and the floor — a mess in the kitchen.

"You're a little upset, I can understand that," Frank said. "But if you'd listen, I said I *knew*, after talking to them, it was a bluff and they'd never go through with it."

"When did you know that," Mickey said, "the first time they called? Monday? How could you possibly know it? A voice on the phone tells you if you don't pay they'll kill your wife."

"That isn't what they said, they'd kill anybody."

"How about, you'll never see your wife again? Are you going to argue about *words?* What were you thinking? Tell me. When you made up your mind you weren't gonna pay."

"I think you're a little hysterical," Frank said. He got a lowball glass from the cupboard, poured vodka into it and dropped in an ice cube.

"There had to be that moment," Mickey said, "when you made the decision."

"I told them right from the beginning I wasn't gonna pay." He raised the glass and drank most of the vodka.

"No, you didn't. You said nothing. For three days, nothing. I want to know what you were thinking."

"I don't believe this," Frank said.

"*You* don't believe it? For Christ sake, Frank, what about *me?* I find out my husband's gonna let somebody kill me and *you* don't believe it."

Frank shook his head, weary but patient. "It wasn't like that at all."

"Did you go to the police?"

"No, I couldn't. They said if I did — that's when they threatened your life."

"I thought you knew it was a bluff."

"It's not — it isn't a simple thing to explain," Frank said. "At first I didn't do anything, I didn't call the police — see? even when you get into that, what police. In Detroit? Freeport? You see what I mean? Because they *did* threaten your life, yes, at that time. But then after, when I talked to them again — where you going?"

Mickey walked to the breakfast table and got a pack of cigarettes from her purse. "Go on, I'm listening." She lit one coming back to the counter.

"So then after, when I talked to them again, I realized it was a bluff and if I didn't do anything, stayed relatively quiet but firm about it, well, by this time I was *convinced* they'd back off. These guys, who are they? Probably somebody, some loser, who used to work for me and was fired. He talks to a couple of friends in a bar — I knew that as soon as I talked to them, I *knew* they'd back off and there was nothing really serious to worry about, outside of course, what you went through — I imagine you had a pretty frightening experience."

"You imagine," Mickey said. "Do you want to imagine it or do you want me to tell you about it?"

"Well, they didn't . . . actually harm you, did they?"

"You mean did they screw me?"

"Jesus Christ," Frank said, "what'd they do?"

"Is it important? I mean would it make any difference?"

"*Yes* it's important. I want to know what happened." Indignant now, his rights on the line.

"I'd like to know something too," Mickey said. "You're not going to tell me, but you know what you did and so do I. So that's all that matters, isn't it?"

"I think after a couple of days — get some rest you'll feel better," Frank said. "When'd you get home, yesterday?"

"You mean when did they let me go? Thursday."

"Well, the reason I ask — since you've been home, has anyone delivered some papers? From the Oakland County Circuit Court." He said then, "You might as well know."

"What kind of papers?" Mickey did know as she said it, as she saw his bland expression, as though he had nothing to hide — the son of a bitch, instead of coming right out and telling her.

"Say it, Frank."

"I'm trying to tell you — last Friday before I left, yes, I filed for divorce."

"Before?"

"You gonna tell me you're surprised, with the way things've been? I finally decided if I didn't file, you would."

"Before —" Mickey said. "So when they were talking to you about the money —"

"Now wait a minute," Frank said.

"When they threatened to kill me, you'd already filed for a divorce? God, no wonder."

"No, you're absolutely wrong. That had nothing to do with anything."

He repeated nearly everything he had said about being sure they were bluffing as Mickey wondered if she should sit down. But she also felt like moving, she was excited and it was a strange mixed feeling: one defeating, the other stimulating, as though her feelings and not her mind were giving her a choice. She could play poor-me and wring her hands and roll over, or she could go after the son of a bitch and let him have it. The rotten son of a bitch — but, that was enough of that. It was all right to be mad, furious; God, she had a right to be. But not if she became emotional and cried and played into his hands. (She could hear him say, "Christ, how can you talk to a woman?") There was no other Mickey perched there watching, prompting words the nice Mickey would never say. There was only one Mickey her — the Mickey she wanted to be — and it was about time to let her loose.

She said, "Is that why you went to Freeport? So you'd be gone when I got the — what's it called?"

"I think it's a summons."

"A summons. And you filed last week?"

"Yeah, Friday. If you'd been here, well, you would've been served by now."

She closed her eyes and opened them. He was still there, with still the blank expressionless gaze, never to change, never to know even when he was funny. She imagined telling someone (Louis?) that if she had been here, see, if she hadn't let herself be dragged off and held in a room for three and a half days, she would've been served with the divorce summons. *Summons.* As though she was being accused of something.

She said to Frank, "I'm sorry the guy from the court will have to make another trip."

He said, "Well, I guess they run into that. You don't always find people home."

There, that was the old Frank she knew so well. Mickey said, "No, you don't, do you?" (Did you get that one, Louis? And Louis would say, Is he for real?)

"I wanted you to have time to read it over," Frank said. "Then you can see about a lawyer, if you think you'll need one. I mean before there's any discussion about the settlement."

"I see," Mickey said. "That's what I started to ask, if you sneaked off to be with what's her name, Melanie, while I read the divorce papers."

He seemed to flinch, not expecting her to say the name. "I didn't sneak off. I went down on business."

"Are you gonna marry her?"

"Well, instead of discussing what I feel is personal — I think it was Henry Kissinger who said, 'Never complain, never explain.' " He looked a little smug as he sipped his drink, the son of a bitch.

"It was Henry Ford the Second," Mickey said, "the time he was arrested in California for drunk driving, with another woman in the car. Did you bring your girlfriend with you or not?"

"I just said, I'm not gonna discuss it."

"Okay, then let's see," Mickey said, "You think I should get a lawyer, huh?"

"Unless you want to use mine," Frank said. "They do that sometimes, people getting a divorce, when the settlement's agreeable to both parties. Saves expenses."

"Who's your lawyer?"

"Sheldon. The one I use."

"Your *business* lawyer?"

"He's a good man."

Mickey said, "Frank, you're too much." (Louis would say, Jesus Christ, he must think you're a fucking moron.)

Frank seemed to be having trouble: frowning, trying to figure her out, her tone, and still maintain an open, honest expression. He said, "I'm trying to do it without strain or pain, if you're willing to cooperate."

"Yes, but how do I know you aren't trying to screw me?" Mickey said.

It stopped him cold for a moment. "Why would I do that?"

"What *is* the settlement?" Mickey said. "What exactly do I get?"

"Well, basically what it is, we sell the house and divide the equity, which is close to two-hundred thousand. Plus, there's alimony and child support. I'm not gonna fight over Bo. I don't think that's fair to him, have to make him choose. So you don't have to worry about that."

"How much alimony?" Mickey said.

"Two thousand a month."

"Are you serious?"

"Am I *serious,* that's twenty-five grand a year. Plus child support, 200 a month. I pay for school, his college, his tennis, within reason."

"How about your business?" Mickey said. "FAD Homes. What's that worth?"

Frank shook his head and said patiently, "No, you see, I derive my income from the business, and out of that I pay the alimony and child support. That's the way it works."

Okay, now.

"And we divide the money you've been sneaking into the Freeport account?"

It didn't have the effect she wanted. Frank paused, but he was ready. He didn't ask her what she was talking about or look puzzled. He said, "There is no Freeport bank account in my name and no possible way anyone can prove there is. If you heard some kind of wild story or speculation, that's all it is."

"I'll bet somebody could cause you a lot of trouble though."

"No way," Frank said.

"Maybe not anybody," Mickey said, "but I bet *I* could."

Frank came close to smiling. "You want to look at my books?"

"No, but I'll look at your apartment buildings and the refrigerators and ranges, all the appliances."

Frank said, "I don't own apartment buildings."

"What if the person you bought all the stuff from was arrested and identified as a kidnapper on top of everything else? Are you following me?"

Frank was not smiling now. He stood very straight, his hands on the counter, and still insisted, trying to give it some conviction, "You can't prove anything."

"But if I started talking to people about it, all your apartment buildings, how you save on stolen materials and stuff, how you pay your old buddy Ray Shelby to front for you — without even getting into the kidnapping I could probably stir up enough to nail your ass," Mickey said mildly, "couldn't I? I mean if I were that type of person and wanted to see you go to jail."

She had him and knew it with a feeling of pure satisfaction. He could protest, deny, make sounds, shrug and shake his head, fool with his glass, but she had him — Mr. Wonderful, the country club champ, scared to death his wife was going to turn him in.

She waited a moment before saying, "Frank?" Quietly.

"What?"

"Are you gonna marry what's her name?"

He was looking down at his glass. "I hope to."

"You mean if you don't go to jail?"

"*No,* I don't mean that."

"Frank, to put your mind at ease," Mickey said, "I don't want any of your Freeport money. And I'm not gonna tell on you . . . I don't think. That's something you'll have to live with." He began to protest again about nothing anyone could prove and she waved it aside. "If you say so, Frank. But there is a question about the settlement. You said 2,000 a month?"

"Well, that's what the lawyer put down."

"It's low, Frank. You want to try again?"

"What were you thinking, around 3,000?"

"I guess we're wasting time," Mickey said. "Let's wait till I get a lawyer."

"That's fine, but if you go out and get an expensive divorce lawyer, just remember," Frank said, "it comes out of the settlement and there's only so much in the kitty. Otherwise I don't give a shit who you get."

Mickey almost smiled, for the first time since she walked in. She said, "Watch it, spunky. There's always Freeport."

He asked Mickey if she was going to open that can of worms again and reminded her that you can't get blood out of a turnip. He was moving out and she could have the house until they agreed on a settlement. Mickey watched him pour a splash of vodka and finish it. He was trying to come back up, regain some of his swagger. Well, let him, she thought. He was the original Frank Dawson — considerably less than he appeared to be — and what's her name could have him.

Frank said, "Can I ask you something?"

"Sure, go ahead."

"Did they, you know, rape you or anything like that?"

Mickey shook her head. "Unh-unh."

"Something happened to you," Frank said, "you're different." He walked out.

Mickey went to the breakfast table and picked up her purse, then walked to the doorway that opened on the front hall and stood facing the stairway, looking up. About fifteen seconds passed before Frank's voice came down from the bedroom.

"What the hell happened to my closet!"

The jerk.

Louis picked up the phone. He said Hello and then said, "Hey, it is, isn't it? I don't believe it. How're you doing?" He listened, nodding, "Yeah, I finally found out a few things. Really crazy, the whole thing. Weird." He listened again and looked over at the coffee table that was still littered with debris, with crusts of pizza and the carry-out box, beer cans, napkins, dirty glasses, ashtrays full of cigarette butts and roaches, the box of Halloween masks,

Mickey's bra . . . "Yeah, it's here . . . Sure, no, it's no trouble at all. No inconvenience. Are you kidding? . . . Fine, okay then."

He walked over to the coffee table, fished Mickey's bra out of the debris, then walked around to the La-Z-Boy where Melanie was lying in a halter top and cut-offs, long brown legs following the contour of the chair, her eyes closed. Louis lifted her hand by the wrist and removed the joint from between her fingers. It was dead. When he dropped her hand on her tummy again, Melanie half opened her eyes.

"Fire inspector," Louis said. "Go back to sleep." He went out to the kitchen.

Ordell was standing at the stove holding an iron skillet of mushrooms with a big mitten, smoke rising out of the pan.

"Turn your fire down. It's too hot."

"How long you cook these things?"

"Few minutes," Louis said. "You don't cook 'em, you get em hot."

"Big girl say yeah, she knows how to cook. She either in the bed or the reclining chair," Ordell said. He glanced toward Louis, his eyes going from the bra Louis was holding to Louis' face, then looked at him again and saw Louis' expression, the man waiting to be asked something, but not wanting to answer.

Ordell knew. He said, "You don't tell me. That was her called?"

Louis nodded. "Honest to God."

"She coming right *here?*" Ordell began to grin.

"We don't know enough yet," Louis said. "What do we know? The broad's stoned since she's been here." He seemed edgy.

"We know," Ordell said. He was still grinning a little.

Louis looked over at the stove. "You're burning your mushrooms."

23

Louis was waiting on the sidewalk in front of the apartment building, looking toward Woodward Avenue and the 6-o'clock traffic. The sun was still hot. He'd been sleepy most of the day, had smoked a couple of joints with Ordell and the big girl; now he felt like moving, doing something. He was excited and tried to stand still.

When he saw Mickey's Grand Prix turn the corner he stood at the curb and raised his hand as the car rolled by — she saw him — noticing the scraped sheetmetal and the fastener holes where the side molding belonged. He walked down and waited as she backed into a parking place, then, as she turned the engine off, opened the door for her.

"I don't believe it," Louis said.

"Who does?" Mickey said.

He stepped back to look at her, making a little show of it. "I thought you were so anxious to change your clothes."

"I *did.* White pants look alike, but this is striped."

"I remember," Louis said. "The one you had on was like a work shirt, light blue. And no bra?"

"I've got a bra on. I have more than one bra," Mickey said. "But I'll tell you something — You hear that?"

"What?"

"That, 'I'll tell you something.' I sound like you."

"I say that?" Louis' face was composed; he seemed very happy, relaxed. But he was looking toward Woodward and holding back a little as they approached the apartment building.

"The something I want to tell you — I really didn't come to pick up the bra."

"You didn't?"

"I felt like talking. I *feel* like talking, and I don't have anybody to talk to who really understands me, I don't think."

"You got to e-*nun*-ci-ate your words," Louis said.

"They don't see things the same way I do or something. I don't know what it is, but I feel like talking and having a drink, one of those things you made. Is that all right, to invite myself?"

"Sure it is, but there's one problem."

"I talked to my husband — well, it was a couple of hours ago, and I got antsy, I couldn't sit around or watch television, I had to talk to somebody . . . What problem? I know — Ordell's back."

"Ordell and somebody else."

"No, really? They're together?" Mickey stopped and Louis turned to stay with her.

"The way things've been going," Louis said, "How can you be surprised at anything?"

"But why would they be together? Didn't she come with my husband?"

"She said your old man went home, wants to start over with you."

"He told her that?" Puzzled. "He wants a divorce. He hasn't changed his mind."

"I don't know, it's what she says. Listen, this broad could tell you anything. Opens these big blue eyes —"

"How old is she?"

"I don't know. Twenty-one."

"She have, you know, big boobs?"

"Nice size."

"My husband, he even wants to marry her. I asked him and he said yes. He said, 'I hope to.' The asshole. I forgot to call him that."

"You don't want him to marry her?"

"*No,* I don't care. He's an asshole whatever he does. God, you can't imagine how good I feel, relieved. It's like I've been tied to him with a heavy rope and finally I got loose."

"I was thinking," Louis said, "you want to talk, we can go to a bar somewhere, have a drink."

She thought about it and bit at her thumbnail looking toward Woodward Avenue and hearing the traffic, feeling the heat and the air close, unmoving. She was not used to the feeling, being in a city in the summertime. She was aware of experiencing something different and caught glimpses in her mind of tenement fire-escapes and men in their undershirts and whores in satin dresses on Gene Kelly's 10th Avenue, a way whores would never look, but the glimpses were real in her mind, stimulating. She felt there was a great deal she'd been missing and had to see.

"I'd like to meet her," Mickey said.

Melanie was reaching from the La-Z-Boy to the coffee table for a can of Coke. Head down, hair hanging, she held the pose to look over as the door opened.

Ordell was sitting across from her, hands folded in his lap, smiling a little, being pleasant.

He said, "Hey, Mickey. How you doing? Louis told me, I said hey, I don't believe it."

Mickey came in, Louis close behind, her glance picking out her bra among the rubble, the same congestion that had covered the table two days ago, before looking at Ordell, at his white teeth in the closely trimmed beard. He reminded her of a desert Arab, not as dark as she thought he'd be in clear light.

"Ordell, right?"

"Yeah," very slow and easy, "sit down. Louis, get the lady something."

She didn't want him to leave her yet. She hadn't looked at the girl, but glanced over now, sinking into the easy chair next to Ordell's, across from the girl.

"Mickey, say hello to Melanie," Ordell said.

"Jesus Christ," Melanie said, pushing up on her elbows a little and tossing her hair from her face.

"Honest to God?"

Mickey said, "I've heard a lot about you." Dumb, but it was an opening. She had to forget about being graded or topped by the girlfriend. The hell with her. She was a big, awkward-looking girl with a lot of unnecessary hair. Size 10 now, but in ten years her boobs would be hanging like melons and she'd be into a fourteen easily. Big girl with broad hips — she could see Frank with Melanie, Frank standing erect, trying to appear taller. The girl's tan legs looked as though they joined her body at her navel, a deep round one; a blond belly dancer.

Melanie was saying she'd heard a lot about Mickey too. (See? Was that so zingy?) Those guys were too much, Melanie said, out of fucking sight.

You can take her, Mickey thought. Why not? She smiled and said, "Well, I was in the neighborhood, I thought why not stop in and see the gang." She looked at Ordell, acting a little dumb. "Is that what you call yourselves, the gang?"

"No, we jes folks here," Ordell said, "don't put on no airs," giving her a little poor nigger, then raised his hands lazily and slapped his palms together, once. "Tell me how yo' hubby is."

"He's jes fine," Mickey said. "If he doesn't get gonorrhea or go to jail, as they say." She wanted to look at Melanie, but couldn't, not yet. She saw Ordell's eyes open a little wider, his grin holding easily.

And heard Melanie say, "Hey, come on, what's

going on? What're you guys doing?"

Louis came in and handed Mickey a tall collins topped with foam and a cherry.

"Louis," Melanie said, "who's your friend? Come on."

Louis brought a chair over from the telephone table in the alcove and sat down next to Mickey. "I thought you were introduced. Melanie, Mickey. Mickey, Melanie."

"Bullshit," Melanie said. "I know what you guys are doing, you're too fucking much, passing this broad off as the wife. You have these routines, you put more into fooling around than you do in . . . whatever you fuckoffs are supposed to do, I haven't a clue to that yet."

Louis sipped his drink, sitting stoop-shouldered in the straight chair, his legs crossed at the knees. "Mickey says her old man's divorcing her." Louis let that hang in the air.

After a moment Ordell said, "You don't tell me."

Mickey said, "I don't want to stand in his way. He has his life, if you want to call it that, and I have mine."

"Say he's divorcing you," Ordell said.

Melanie threw her hair aside. "And then she goes, 'Yes he is,' And then you go, 'Oh, really? For true?' Putting me on, but I like it, it's a kick. So go right ahead."

"I say," Mickey said, "or I *go,* If you don't believe I'm real, do you want me to describe the apartment in Freeport?"

"Ordell's been there," Melanie said. "He could've told you all about it."

"Then I say, Do you want me to describe Frank's liver spot? It's shaped like South America and located two inches west of the base of his spine. I assume you've been there," Mickey said.

"Wow," Melanie said, smiling now. "I thought it looked more like Africa."

"It's probably getting bigger," Mickey said. "I haven't seen it in a while. Does he still march in with a towel over his arm."

"I'm trying to get him to be more spontaneous," Melanie said, "but he's very ritualistic, you know? Goes by the book. I tell him hey, it's all right, but you've been reading the wrong book, man." She squirmed her fanny in the La-Z-Boy. "I got to take a leak."

"Sit still," Ordell said, looking at Melanie. "Man's gonna divorce this lady. It seems he's not going back and start over, is he?"

"So I was wrong," Melanie said. "Call Cedric and get the boat, what do you want me to do? I can't help it if he tells me one thing, he tells her something else. Or she's pissed off, *she's* doing it."

Ordell looked at Mickey. "You mad at anybody?"

"Not really," Mickey said.

"You not mad at us?"

"No, I think it's kinda interesting."

"*In*teresting?" Melanie said. "It's fucking wild. Get Frank here we'll have everybody."

Louis said, "It's different, isn't it?" He looked at Mickey. "Sitting around with friends sure beats doing time."

"You mind terribly?" Melanie said, pushing up out of the chair. "I got to take a leak *now* or never."

Mickey watched her stand up and pull her tight cut-offs out of her fanny. She was unstable, probably stoned, and weaved the first few steps crossing the room to the hall that led to the bathroom.

Mickey said, "Well, there she goes, the next Mrs. Frank Dawson. Looks like a million bucks, doesn't she?"

Ordell said, "He tell you that? He's gonna marry her?"

"And live with her till he does," Mickey said.

"My," Ordell said. "My my my *my*."

"How much you think he likes her?" Louis said.

"A whole bunch," Mickey said. "Call him up and ask him. He's cleaning out his closet."

Ordell looked at Louis as Mickey leaned close to the coffee table to get her bra, picked it up, hesitated, and pulled the cardboard box toward her. She said, "All the other day I kept looking at this. What's in it?"

Louis looked at Ordell.

Melanie came back into the room zipping up, then swinging her hair aside. She stopped, walked over to the hi-fi changer and rows of records and tapes on the wall shelf. She said, "You know who knocks me out? Esther Phillips . . . but I'll settle for Roberta Flack," and was moving her hips to *You've Lost That Loving Feeling* when she turned around and stopped and howled and shook her head and said, "Fucking wild — hey, I want to play too!"

There were three Richard Nixons sitting by the coffee table. One Richard Nixon was holding the telephone in his lap. The second Richard Nixon was holding a Little Orphan Annie mask, placing tape over the round eyeholes. The third Richard Nixon held a notepad and pencil and was writing directions to her grandmother's house that was off by itself on the shores of Lake Huron and had an upstairs bedroom that was just like the one Richard's mother used to live in.

It was hot in the mask. Mickey wished the big girl would hurry up and realize what was happening to her so she could take her bra and leave . . . go home and watch Frank get his phone call.

ISIS publish a wide range of books in large print, from fiction to biography. A full list of titles is available free of charge from the address below. Alternatively, contact your local library for details of their collection of ISIS books.

Details of ISIS unabridged audio books are also available.

Any suggestions for books you would like to see in large print or audio are always welcome.

ISIS
55 St Thomas' Street
Oxford OX1 1JG
(0865) 250333

G G — 27/4/17